RISK IT ALL

ML NYSTROM

HOT TREE PUBLISHING

DRAGON RUNNERS MC

Mute

Stud

Blue

Table

Brick

MACATEER BROTHERS

Run With It

Ready For It

Hold It Close

Risk It All

Give It To Me

For information, contact the publisher, Hot Tree Publishing.

www.hottreepublishing.com

Editing: Hot Tree Editing

Cover Designer: BookSmith Design

Ebook ISBN: 978-1-922359-90-2

Paperback ISBN: 978-1-922359-91-9

To Aileen Geraghty and Olivia Smith. Two of the strongest women I know who can smile and laugh while donning fuzzy hats.

Chapter One

THE WOMAN SCREAMED AND CLUTCHED AT PATRICK's head between her legs. He rapid-fired his tongue over her hard clit and she came with a long keening sound. He paused long enough to roll on a condom before he lifted himself over her still writhing body and slid his hard cock inside her. Christ, what a feeling! Warm, wet, wonderful pussy. He pulled out and drove in again, a mewling cry of pleasure coming from her throat. His own groan echoed hers as he set a steady pace, thrusting in and out. She ran her long, decorated nails down his sweaty back and grabbed his ass cheeks with both hands.

"Harder, baby. Harder," she gasped in his ear. "Oh, yes, give me more!"

He started pounding, the sound of slapping wet

flesh eclipsing her wild cries. Faster and faster he drove his hips into her body, and she grabbed him tighter. He winced as one of her claws scratched his skin enough to hurt.

"Ah, lass, ease up a bit."

She didn't.

She squeezed and slapped his ass, screaming and making noises at the same time. It stung, distracting him. Pulling her arms up to her ears, he anchored them there while he hammered away. His balls tightened and his groin tingled. *Ah, almost here. Almost. Gahhh!*

He buried himself one last time, pushing as deep as he could, and shot his load into the latex sheath. Blood rushed to his head, and he fell on top of the woman as he came. Sweat made their skin slick, and she continued to thrash under him.

"Yeah, baby. More! Don't stop."

Christ, she hadn't figured out yet he'd finished. He waited a heartbeat or two before pulling out and striding to the small bathroom the motel sported. The yellowed walls might have been white during the last century, but the sink and shower worked. For temporary lodgings, that was enough.

Patrick stripped off the spent condom and tied it in a knot before throwing it in the plastic-lined trash can. Two others were already sitting at the bottom from the last couple of nights, which indicated the diligence of the housekeeping staff. He wiped off his dick with one of the rough white washcloths and wondered if he should take one to... Jamie? Jane? Janice? Fuck, he'd already forgotten her name. He dropped the cloth to the floor to join the towel he left there this morning. If she wanted to clean up, she could get her ass out of bed and go in the bathroom herself.

He sauntered back into the cheap room, his heavy dick swinging between his legs, and smiled at the blonde still flat on her back, legs spread. Her rounded breasts sporting large rosy nipples bore the love bites from where he'd sucked on them earlier. Wide hips, soft stomach, and bare pussy completed the scene. She really was a pretty woman, even with her makeup smeared from hard fucking. His dick twitched with renewed mild interest. "All right, love?"

Rhythmic thumping came from the other side of the wall. Patrick knew it was his identical twin, Angus, getting it on with the woman's friend. Carla? Carrie? Corrie? He was really bad with names.

"Yeah, I'm good. Real good, baby." She lifted her breasts with her hands. "Maybe could be better?"

Patrick shrugged and picked up his pack of cigarettes and a lighter from the flimsy nightstand. "Might have another go in a bit. Not a young 'un anymore, love. Takes me a wee minute to get hard for a second round."

She giggled. "I just love your accent. Where you from again?"

Ha, gets them every time. Patrick had figured out a long time ago, if he dropped a few Irish-sounding words, the ladies would drop their panties. "I was born here in America, but me family came from the old country across the pond."

Her glazed eyes said she didn't get the reference, but it didn't matter, anyway. Tomorrow, she could boast to her friends that she got to fuck a man from another country, and he got his night's entertainment. Win-win, right?

Patrick ignored the No Smoking sign for the room and tapped out a slim white stick. It wasn't a daily habit for him—more like weekly or just after a nice, long fuck. He and Angus had lucked out getting these dirt-cheap rooms that rented by the week. Up in this area of Pennsylvania, accommodations were scarce and finding something short-term turned out to be challenging. The Barett Motel had been around for decades, and based on the décor, stuck in the 70s. At least the owners put in those small refrigerator/microwave combination appliances, making the rooms livable enough for a brief stay.

Patrick lit up the cigarette, took a big puff, and ignored the blonde on the bed who watched him. Jackie? Jasmine? Janet? Gah. If he just kept calling her "lass" and "love," maybe she wouldn't figure out he'd forgotten her name.

The thumping stopped with a dual shout through the thin wall from Angus and the other woman. Patrick grinned, wondering if Angus got his wish of some backdoor action. The few times they'd shared, Angus always took the ass while Patrick got the pussy. He didn't quite understand his brother's fascination with anal sex, but they were different men even if they looked exactly the same.

"Got one of those for me?" The woman sat up, flipping the thin polyester comforter across her lap, but leaving her boobs free to hang down.

Patrick tapped out another white stick and handed it to her, along with the lighter. She sucked in a big lungful and blew smoke rings in the air. "How much longer are you planning on being in town?"

"Another week. Then it's off to a new adventure for me brother and me."

She did that pouty thing that women did with their mouths where they puckered up and stuck out the lower lip. Patrick thought it cute on some women. On this one, the gesture made her look like a six-year-old about to have a tantrum. "Maybe you'd like to stick around for a while."

"Ah, lass, you know me job is a travelin' one. I have to go where the work takes me."

She took in another big puff from the cigarette. "You have another job lined up? Maybe you can find something local?"

Patrick took another hit from his own cigarette. Her words sparked a familiar warning bell in the back of his head. She didn't get this was a one-time thing. Fucking hell, why did women have to do that? This wasn't the first time he'd taken a woman to bed for a simple night of mutual fun. He always made it clear he wanted no obligations or ties. Just a good, hard fuck. Everyone walked away happy, no harm, no foul. If his target for the night said no or indicated she expected more, he moved on to the next one until he found a willing partner who knew the score. If she jumped into bed with him, he made sure she came first, several times if possible, before he took his own pleasure. Afterwards, he expected to be done and no clingy lovey-dovey mess.

He ignored the woman's huffing snit and picked up his phone. It dinged earlier with a message, but being more occupied getting his rocks off, he'd waited to check it. He raised one eyebrow seeing the text came from Connor, his older brother.

Connor: How much longer you and Angus have on the job you're working now in PA?

Patrick let his thumbs runs over the screen.

Patrick: Deadline is at the end of the month, but we're done this Friday.

The three dots bounced around as Patrick inhaled more smoke and blew a cloud into the air.

Connor: I got more work coming in than I can handle. Owen is swamped. Garrett has joined us, and we still can't keep up. If you're up for it, I could use both you and Angus on some jobs. Good money. If you're not booked already, we need the help. Texted Angus too, but he's not answered yet.

Patrick grinned. Connor had no idea how perfect his timing was at that moment. "Sorry, love. Angus and I are heading to North Carolina on Saturday. Our family is in dire need of help and we have to go." He shrugged and finished the cigarette, stubbing it out on a random plastic coffee cup top.

"That's really sweet of you. My family sucks big time."

He grinned even bigger. He got back on the bed and kneeled, straddling the woman's lap. His hand reached down to cup his dick and point it at her. "Well now, lass, speaking of sucking, I bet with a wee bit of help from you, we can go another round sooner rather than later. What do you say?"

If she said she finished for the night, he would have gotten off her, and either waited longer or talked her into leaving. Instead, she smiled and opened her mouth to draw him in deep.

"Ah, yesss, that's my girl." Patrick closed his eyes as the woman's head bobbed on his dick. The thumping from the other room started up again and Patrick smiled. Apparently Angus was up again and getting his own action. Twins forever—they would compare notes later.

Chapter Two

THE LIGHTS FROM THE BAR AND SOUNDS FROM THE Irish band bled outside to the street. Patrick decided St. Paddy himself shone down on him and Angus tonight as he found parking just across from the place.

He shook Angus awake and opened the glove compartment to pull out a stick of Axe deodorant and a comb. "Wake up, brother. We're here."

"Connor's place?" Angus sniffed and stretched.

"No, dumbass. Bevvie said they were goin' out for a bit tonight. Come on. I need to get out of this fucking truck and into a pretty lass. It is my day, after all."

"What the hell are you talking about?"

Patrick slipped the scented stick under his shirt

and swiped it under his armpit. "Angus, what's the date?"

The twin grinned, fully awake now. "Aye, I see what you're saying. St. Paddy's Day."

Patrick grinned back and ran the comb through his thick ginger hair to let it flop over. The fade on either side of his head needed touching up, but he'd deal with that later. "It is our duty, no, our *obligation* to go in there to see family and make our presence known to this city in the biggest, loudest fashion possible."

Angus ran a hand over the shaved sides and the Viking braid on the back of his skull. Both men had similar haircuts but wore it in different styles. It was the only way most people told them apart. "Well then, brother, let's not keep the masses waiting."

Patrick tossed him the deodorant. "Good idea to freshen yourself a bit after ten hours of driving."

Angus caught the stick and applied it as Patrick got out and raised his arms to the night sky in a long bone-cracking stretch. "Let's get this party started, brother."

Patrick strode up to the lit entrance of the pub. The atmosphere of the place gave him a second wind, and he breathed deeply before opening the door. He lifted his hand high, palms out, and spread his legs to take up as much room as possible.

"Bow down, mere mortals! Patrick and Angus are in the hoooooouuuuuse!" His voice rang out and even though the noise kept going, every eye in the place turned in his direction.

"Patrick!" Beverly, his oldest brother's wife, hurried over to him. Melanie, the pretty blonde that Owen somehow had snagged, followed closely behind. He spotted his brothers plus a couple of other women sitting at the bar.

"Ah, me beautiful sister-in-law! Please tell me you've come to your senses and are ready to run away with me?" He put his arms around the stout woman and squeezed her in an enormous hug. *Jesus, Mary, and Joseph, it was good to be in a place that felt like home!*

Beverly hugged him back, then punched him on the shoulder. "Not a chance, little brother. You want a shot or a beer?"

His face feigned horror. "Lass, don't you know me? Both, of course."

Melanie stepped in for her own hug. "Good to see you, Patrick."

"Aye. I can't tell you how good it is to be here." His words held meaning, as he whispered them into her ear. Then the regular Patrick came back. "Now where's my drink?" He slung an arm around either woman as he purposefully dragged them to their spot at the bar.

Angus was more subdued as he followed the trio. "I'm so dry, dust would go down easy."

The bartender set down two whiskey shots and two green beers for the newcomers. Patrick eyed the woman with the long blonde hair tipped in green. She was thin, painfully so with hardly any breasts or ass at all. Pretty blue-gray eyes met his as he picked up the small glass in one hand and the beer in the other. Angus did the same. "Life, liberty, and the pursuit of happiness. *Sláinte!*"

"*Sláinte!*" Garrett, Connor, and Owen had switched to beer. Glasses clinked and lifted. Patrick turned to the youngest woman who appeared to be a part of the group, but someone he hadn't met before. A big flirty smile plastered itself across his face. "So, is your name Happiness?"

The woman giggled and ducked her head. *Score!* Patrick thought as he took a hefty drink of the green beer.

Too bad Melanie had to intervene. "Don't you try anything with this one, Patrick MacAteer. You either, Angus." She turned to face the petite female. "Fair warning, sister. These two are the biggest horn-dogs God ever put on this planet. I wouldn't take anything they say seriously."

Patrick pretended to get hurt. He put a hand over his heart and made a gulping sound. "Shot dead. Oh, cruel, cruel woman! You'll dance over me grave at midnight, won't you?"

"Absolutely, if you fuck with my friend here."

Angus put his empty shot glass on the bar and took a big swig of beer. "Ah now, lass. We won't fuck *with* your friend."

The stink-eye Melanie shot him should have burned the man to a cinder. Melanie used to be one of the biggest party-girls in Asheville until she became a mother and hooked up with Owen.

Patrick chuckled at her words. No doubt she caught Angus's subtle play on words. The funny part was Melanie's eye lasers had no effect on Angus as he turned his full attention to the small brunette. "What's your name?"

"I'm Rhyleigh Givens. Part owner of the yoga place, along with Melanie and Bertie."

Bertie, eh? Must be the one standing next to Garrett. Patrick picked up on the name he'd heard so often in his calls with Beverly. Connor talked to him man-to-man, but Bevvie shared all the family gossip. His older brother, Garrett, had recently escaped from a toxic relationship with a woman who all but sucked him dry. He'd moved to Asheville to get away from her and to heal. In the process, he met Bertie and jumped right back into a serious relationship.

Patrick looked at the pretty woman and could see why Garrett chose to be with her, but that didn't mean she was good for his older brother. He smiled, but his protective instinct kicked in as he greeted her. "You're Bertie, then? Garrett's Bertie? Nice to meet you. Connor tells us you're not a raving lunatic bitch like the last one."

"Here now, Patrick. Watch your tongue." Garrett bristled.

Patrick raised an eyebrow at his brother's tone. The woman in question diffused the situation by smiling and sticking out her hand. "Yes, I'm Bernadette, or Bertie for short. And no, I'm not a raving lunatic. Bitch only when necessary."

Patrick paused for a half-second. Her words and her manner told him a lot. Her confidence and calm stated I-have-a-place-here-and-you're-not-taking-it-from-me. Couple that with Garrett's defensive stance, meant there might be another sister-in-law in the future. *Damn, another MacAteer bites the dust!* He threw his head back and roared with laughter.

He ignored the hand and enfolded Bertie in a big bear hug. "Great to meet you, lass. It's about time Garrett found himself a good one. Fuck me sideways, I'm always late to the party. Barkeep! Another round!"

"None for us, Sloane. We need to get going." Melanie put her empty glass on the bar and Sloane whisked it away as she poured another round of shots.

Patrick watched the woman's constant motion. She might be small, but she was strong. Each pour filled the small glasses with exact amounts straight from the bottle. No drips or spills. It was clear she'd been behind this bar for a long time. She smiled at customers and did some cute bartender tricks of flipping glasses, twirling tongs around her finger, and bouncing caps off her elbow into the trash can.

"It's early yet," Angus protested. He picked up his colored drink and swallowed a good portion of it. "Patrick and I have to catch up a wee bit."

"Aye, that we do." Patrick quietly agreed as he reached out to snag one of the newly poured shots. Sloane raised her eyes to meet his, and he winked at her as he tossed the liquor to the back of his throat. Instead of the flirty wink back he expected, she scowled at him. "You starting a tab or mooching off Connor's?"

Patrick let the woman's ire bounce off him and turned the small glass over. He pushed toward her with one finger. "Tab, me darlin'. Name's Patrick MacAteer."

She stopped working for a minute and gaped at him. "Another one? How many of you are there?"

Patrick leaned on the bar with his elbows and ticked them off. "Connor is the oldest. Owen and Garrett are twins, but fraternal. I think Owen came first, but I can't remember. Angus and I are next and we're identical. We had to start wearing our hair differently so people could tell us apart. He's the oldest by about twenty minutes. I'm the youngest brother, but we have a younger sister, Eva. She's married to a biker and lives in Bryson City. Ever hear of the Dragon Runners MC?"

Sloane dropped her eyes and resumed her work. "Yeah, I know of them. Good people. I take my car to Ditchdigger's place. He's part of the local chapter." She lifted the spouted bottle high and aimed a stream right into the glass. Perfect pour. Impressive.

Patrick lifted the fresh shot and threw it back in one go. The fire from the first one had already settled into a slow glowing burn in his stomach. The greasy drive-through burger from a few hours ago had long since disappeared and he briefly thought he needed to take it easy. *Fuck no, I'm drinking tonight! That's what Ubers are for.*

"If yoor havin' trouble, lass, I'll be glad to look under the hood for yoo." He accompanied the thinly veiled suggestion with a half-smile and another wink. His added accent thickened as he turned on the bedroom charm and turned it up to eleven.

Again the woman surprised him with her reaction. Instead of demurring and making a play of her own, she rolled her eyes and affected her own Irish brogue. "Ah now, laddie, ya think me daft? I have a bar full of thirsty people and no time for yoor blarney. If me hood needs anything, I'll tend it later meself."

She winked back at him and turned away to take another order.

For once, Patrick was speechless.

Melanie's voice grabbed his attention. "We have a babysitter who's probably watching the clock about now. Love that you guys are here. Talk business and shit. We'll see you tomorrow at lunch, yes?"

Patrick put the cute acidic bartender out of his mind and bear-hugged his brother's woman. "Feed me and you'll be my favorite," he remarked as he released Melanie.

"Beverly's cooking. I can't boil water without burning it."

Patrick laughed as his brother had informed him about some of Melanie's kitchen disasters. He let the rest of the conversation float around him as he wasn't too interested in the lunch plans for the next few days. He was too busy watching the bartender stack a bunch of silver shakers and pour five drinks at once. Damn, she was good.

He noticed Angus sidle up to the pretty yoga woman. His twin offered her a seat and set himself behind her as if staking a claim. *Renee? Ripley? Reina? Shit, I forgot already.* That left Patrick as the only one there without a woman. Fuck that! Patrick snatched another shot from the row of shots and slammed it back. The bartender growled at him, but he ignored the sound and blew her a kiss.

"Party poopers, the lot of ya. Come, me true loves, dance with me before I grow roots." He grabbed yoga woman and Bertie and dragged them to the dance floor. If some people found his behavior obnoxious, he really didn't care. He worked hard and played harder and if they didn't like it, well, fuck 'em.

He gave the pretty yoga woman a sideways smile and glance. "My beautiful new girlfriend, please don't leave me!"

She laughed as she danced with him. "I'm not your girlfriend."

"Oh, but you want to be. I'm cuter than Angus, you know."

"I thought you were identical?"

"We are, but I'm still the cute one."

The band started playing their next song and Patrick's eyes lit up like firecrackers. So many shots in his stomach had stripped away any inhibitions he might have had about being in a new town and a new place. "Holy shit, I love this song!"

No one in the band protested when he hopped on stage to join in. He danced and sang at the top of his lungs. Even buzzed, he managed to get through the rapid complicated lyrics of "The Rattlin' Bog." The audience appreciated the skillful show and gave him a big round of applause as he took an exaggerated bow and jumped from the stage. Bertie left to go back to Garrett, but several other women joined him. *I have my own fan club going here,* he thought as he gyrated and smiled and flirted and charmed.

Yoga-girl matched him dance for dance, but she gave up after a while and took a break to sit at the table his brothers commandeered. A pretty blonde twerked in front of him, and he watched her pumping butt with interest. He and Angus had checked into a cheap room for the night for the both of them, and it wouldn't be the first time they both brought women back, one for each bed. They had even switched places once to see if the women noticed.

They didn't.

The band sang their final song and said good night. Most of the dance floor and indeed the pub had emptied, and only a few hard-core partiers were left. It surprised Patrick that his older brothers were still around as they had families to get home to. Then again, it had been a long time since they'd been together.

He galloped up to the bar, sweating from the physical exertion and high on life. "Oy, what a night! Great music. Barkeep! A pint of your finest!"

"Last call happened twenty minutes ago," she called back without looking up from her work.

"Ah please, my lovely lass, just one wee pint to quench me parched throat."

She frowned at him. "Nope."

He smiled big and wheedled. "Please, darlin'? I'm

new in town and I'm lookin' for a warm, wet welcome."

Sloane stopped her work and looked straight into his eyes. By the annoyed look on her face, she was not impressed. Mild intrigue filled Patrick. He usually got what he wanted with a little cajoling and flattery. Seldom had his charm and good looks not worked on a woman. The stare down grew longer, and heat burned on the back of Patrick's neck. This woman had no intention of giving in and for the first time, Patrick feared he met his match.

Then she flipped the towel she's been using over her shoulder and crossed her arms over her small chest. "I'll give you a beer in a bottle for the road if you stand on that table and sing 'Danny Boy' so I can post it on the Facebook page."

Patrick grinned in relief. Both for the release from her intense eyes and that he knew the song well. "Challenge accepted!" He climbed up and caught his balance. She took out her phone to film. He placed his hand over his heart and assumed a dramatic pose while he began to sing.

> *"Oh Danny boy, the pipes, the pipes are calling*
> *From glen to glen, and down the mountainside*
> *The summer's gone, and all the roses falling*
> *'Tis you, 'tis you must go and I must bide."*

Another voice joined in and Patrick recognized Angus harmonizing with him.

"But come ye back when summer's in the meadow
Or when the valley's hushed and white with snow
'Tis I'll be here in sunshine or in shadow
Oh Danny boy, oh Danny boy, I love you so."

Patrick thought Connor had fallen asleep at the table until he stood and joined his brother with a deep baritone. A twinge hit Patrick's heart as he sorted through a few memories of the brothers all singing together. There had been many times as children when that was their only form of entertainment. They had spent most of their lives traveling from job to job with their father and working on the family construction crew. Campgrounds, the family RV, and temporary accommodations were more the norm than having a house or a home. Many times TV was not available.

"But when he come, and all the flowers are dying
If I am dead, as dead I well may be
You'll come and find the place where I am lying
And kneel and say an 'Ave' there for me."

A few patrons still hanging around came over and sang with the impromptu performance or hummed the tune if they didn't know the words. Patrick closed his eyes at the sight and sound and let his voice ring loud and high. The alcohol still ran through his system, making him somewhat maudlin.

"And I shall hear, tho' soft you tread above me
And all my grave will warm and sweeter be
For you will bend and tell me that you love me
And I shall sleep in peace until you come to me."

Silence met his ears after the last notes faded. Patrick's heart dipped, and the shock of tears in his eyes made him sober up.

The sound of a single person clapping came from the bar. The bartender held out two handfuls of cold bottles. "Take 'em home before you open them, boys. Now that's how you close down a pub."

The patrons took the offered bottles with thanks as Patrick hopped down from his perch. Congratulatory back slaps and a chorus of "nice job" and "great voice" greeted him as he picked his own bottle of cold, wet beer and twisted off the cap. His intention was to drain the bottle dry in one go; however, he stopped when he saw the woman's reflection in the bar mirror.

She turned away to straighten the liquor bottles on the back-wall display. Tension pulled her muscles into rigid ropes. She hid herself from the celebrating bar and no one paid attention to the two tears tracking down her cheek. A thin hand came up to wipe them away and Patrick could see the fatigue on her face. Patrick kept his eyes on the struggling woman. He watched her bite her lip in an effort to keep it still and regain control.

Something about the song or the rough night? She had been on her feet serving, pouring, cleaning, and ringing up orders for the bar and the waitresses since before he and Angus showed up and Patrick hadn't seen her sit down. Not once. He admired she had the power and energy to keep up all night. Long workdays were normal for him as well, but he was a lot bigger and stronger than this tiny woman.

Sloane. Sloane was her name.

As if sensing his perusal, she lifted her eyes and met his in the mirror. Her tears dried up, and she lifted an eyebrow at him in a classic what-the-hell-do-you-want expression. He smiled and winked at her before he lifted the bottle in a private toast and tipped it back.

Chapter Three

"Look out, Sloane. Incoming cougar."

I groaned at Gordon's warning as I spotted Maggie Garfield walking in the door this Thursday night. She wore a short red dress on her generous hour-glass figure and her highest fuck-me pumps. There was no doubting her intentions for coming out tonight. Her husband, Sean, must be out of town, leaving her to prowl.

My mouth turned down in a long frown as she seated herself on a stool and flipped her dark hair. Cheating on Sean was a regular occurrence when she had the opportunity. I hated it, but I had no say in what my patrons did in their private lives. I just pulled drafts, made drinks, and took their money. The only time I interfered was if something went down here at the bar. Sexual harassment happened occasionally to my female patrons, and when it did, I put the kibosh on it as quickly as possible. My reputation as a no-nonsense person had grown, and very few people messed with me about it.

Gordon kept his back to me, tacitly refusing to serve the woman. I couldn't blame him as the few times he had, she came on to him, and he didn't like that at all. He wanted to ban her ass, but we didn't have a good reason other than her blatant infidelity. If we banned everyone who came to the bar for a one-night hookup, we'd go bankrupt in a month.

I tossed my ever-present dish towel over my shoulder and approached the woman. Her eyes were so busy checking out the field, I had to clear my throat to get her attention. She seemed disappointed to see me instead of Gordon. Too bad, so sad.

"Hi, Maggie. What can I get you?" I cringed, knowing what she would order.

"I need a screaming orgasm, pronto." Her voice rang loud and clear.

I swear whoever named this drink did it solely for the purpose of fucking with bartenders. If she didn't find a victim soon, she'd be ordering other drinks with sex names. Buttery nipples, leg spreaders, blow jobs, and whatever else she found on the internet that could get her noticed and annoy the shit out of me.

I poured vodka, Baileys, Kahlua, and cream into a shaker just as Patrick showed up. He and his brother had come in the bar nearly every night since they showed up last week. The Facebook post of him singing on top of the table had garnered more had been watched a bazillion times already and some women had come to the bar specifically to find him.

"Greetings, my favorite people!" He wore his typical uniform of jeans, boots, and a dark green Henley with the sleeves pushed up. "Sloane, my love, I'm dying for a drink. Can you pull me a Green Man?"

"Lager or IPA?"

"Lager, darlin'. Love the red hair."

A little thrill spun in my chest at his compliment. I had to tell myself over and over again that his attention didn't mean anything, but I did enjoy his notice. His order for the lighter beer told me he drove by himself tonight. Guinness meant Angus came with him, and Jameson whiskey meant someone else would take him home. He impressed me by being that responsible about driving after drinking and knowing his limits.

I finished pouring the creamy drink for Maggie

into a short ball glass and set it in front of her. She ignored it as her eyes stapled to the handsome ginger-haired man shaking hands and slapping backs.

"Who's that?" I swear I could smell the pheromones floating from her pores.

I pulled a large beer mug and tilted it to fill from the tap. "That's Patrick." I felt no other need to explain.

"Patrick." Her breathy voice told me she had found her prey.

I wanted to throw the cold beer at her head. Maybe that would cool her ass down a bit.

Patrick came to the bar and picked up the mug. His hair fade seriously needed a trim and he'd pulled the long locks on the top of his head back into a loose bun at the back. It gleamed wetly from a recent shower.

"Sloane, you're my absolute favorite." He grinned and winked at me before taking a big slurp.

I admit it. My belly fluttered, and I had to quell the urge to titter. Ugh. Me. Tittering. What a joke. That flutter lasted about three seconds as he turned to the drooling woman beside him.

"And who might you be, pretty lady?"

I didn't stick around to listen to Maggie's reply or

the subsequent conversation of heavy sexual innu-endos. I had a bar to run and booze to sell. Nope, I was not envious of the attention. Not me.

True to form, Patrick talked, smiled, winked, and bought Maggie several more drinks. I had to look up what was in a suck-bang-n-blow cocktail and ended up substituting some ingredients for what I didn't have on hand. Herbal liqueur? Really?

A few hours later, I saw Patrick put a giggling fucked-up Maggie into an Uber. Then he came back and ordered another beer. I tried. I did, but I couldn't help myself.

"Too drunk or too old?" I asked when he sat back down, and I set the fresh beer in front of him.

"Too married. Not a place I'll go." He took a big drink and slumped over the bar as if his energy finally ran out.

I wiped the top and collected some dirties to put in the washer underneath the counter. He stayed silent for a change, showing me a side of him I'd not seen. It surprised me as the exuberant ladies' man full of loud life and good times had always been at the forefront anytime he'd been at my bar.

"Maggie's been here before looking for action. What tipped you off?"

He put the glass on the bar, placed his elbows around it, and ticked off his points finger by finger.

"One, there is an indentation where her wedding rings sits. Dead giveaway. Two, she slipped up and said her husband's name. I let it go, but I heard it. Third, she worked it way too hard. Ordering sex drinks, pulling at her skirt, licking her lips. Classic plays. Besides that, she wasn't looking for a good time. That woman is desperate for attention from someone. Even a stranger at a bar. Whoever her husband is, he spends more time doing other things than taking care of his wife."

He shrugged and picked up his half-drunk glass for another long pull. "She needs a long, hard fuck, but more than that, she needs to feel like a woman should. Admired, desired, and appreciated. I gave her that without compromising her vows."

I hummed a response. "Nice of you to do that, Patrick. I figured you'd be in bed with her an hour ago."

He lifted one corner of his mouth. "Aye, I could have, but there are some lines I won't cross. Way too many complications and Clara would be one of them."

"You mean Maggie."

He grinned and picked up his beer. "Yeah, Maggie."

I needed to perhaps reassess my opinion of him. There was more depth to the Irish boy toy than I thought.

He finished the beer and reached out to tweak a piece of my bright red locks. "You know, Sloane, you could've told me about her."

My belly surprised the hell out of me by flipping when he reached out to touch me. I also noted that he never forgot my name. Even though that idea gave me warm fuzzies, I wasn't naïve enough to think it meant anything. He'd been coming in often enough he damn well better know who served him and put up with his shenanigans. I covered my reaction by flipping the mass over my shoulder along with the dishtowel. "And spoil a good show? Believe me, baby, the shit that goes on here is better than any reality program."

He looked straight into my eyes, and for a moment, my heart stopped beating. Then he threw his head back and roared with laughter. Patrick was back to normal.

My alarm blared, and I reluctantly got up to face the day. Ten might seem late to some people, but since I crawled into bed around four thirty, I still only got about five and a half hours of sleep, and that was on a good night. If lucky, I'd be able to take a nap later should I get an opportunity. Wishful thinking on my part, but there was always hope.

Patrick left before I made last call. After the bar closed, my work didn't end. Cleanup, receipts, running the day's financial report, cashing out the register, and carrying the deposit bags up to my loft apartment over the building. All of that needed finishing before I could rest. I had the top-floor unit, which was smaller, but came with a cool outdoor deck area on the roof. My brother, Gordon, had the big second-floor unit along with his girlfriend and daughter.

I dressed and made coffee in my tiny kitchen. No need to shower as I'd done that when I staggered up the steps after work. After slinging booze all night, I always felt nasty from being covered in dried sweat and bar goo. No way could I crawl into my nice clean bed that way.

During the week, the bar opened at four and closed at midnight, but on weekends, we opened at two and closed at two. We had a couple of waitresses on weekends and party nights, but Gordon and I did most of the work. This kept our overhead as low as possible and so far we stayed in the black, but it wouldn't take a lot for that needle to slip over to the red.

We co-owned the business. But for mortgage and credit purposes, my name was on the building. The original idea I had in purchasing instead of leasing was to rent the two apartments to cover the loan payments. The revenue from the bar would pay for its own expenses and make a nice profit. Didn't quite work the way I expected. Asheville is not a cheap place to live; therefore, we decided it didn't make sense for someone to pay us rent, while we had to pay rent ourselves for separate living quarters. As of now, the bar's earnings covered all expenses and had enough profits for us to collect small salaries. We managed to produce a decent living, though not a rich one.

After coffee, I munched on a Pop-Tart and opened my laptop to catch up on the books. Once a quarter, I had an accountant come in to straighten out anything I'd missed and file taxes. Otherwise, I handled the day-to-day money. The bank bag sat on my kitchen table and I counted coins, tattered bills, and credit card receipts. Most people ran a tab on plastic, but there were always a smattering of locals who preferred cash. I picked up a one-hundred-dollar bill that had a phone number scribbled on it along with a smear of red lipstick.

Automatically, my mind shot straight to Patrick MacAteer.

Almost two weeks had passed since the St. Patrick's Day party and he'd become a regular customer. Angus came with him most nights, but a few times, the handsome party man came by himself. I swear he had to be the biggest, most outrageous flirt ever born. No woman was immune to him, at least none that I'd seen, and being female was the only requirement. Big, small, tall, short, blonde, brunette, he turned on that supernova smile of his and panties dropped. From the bar talk I'd overheard, he'd nailed more than one woman already and broken a few hearts along the way. One girl wailed to her companions that he called her Arianna twice when her name was Maudie.

I popped the rest of my breakfast in my mouth and stacked up last night's receipts. Patrick MacAteer was not my problem. He was gorgeous, built like a brick house, and exceedingly fun to be around, but definitely a prize that the single female population wanted to land. His smile had enough power in it to even charm me a little. Already I'd found myself laughing and teasing back with him as we got to know each other.

I discovered he did have some scruples though. Last night, I watched him reject a guaranteed night in bed with a more-than-willing woman. Perhaps there was more to him than the manwhore image he put out.

The sudden loud banging on my door scared the piss out of me, and I dropped the hundred-dollar bill on the table.

"Sloane? You up?"

Gordon didn't wait but came straight into my loft. "You have coffee? Cammie forgot to get it yesterday. She's not feelin' too well the last few days."

I gestured toward my kitchen. "Whole pot full. Help yourself."

"Thanks. Bar did good last night?"

"Good for a Thursday." I placed the stacked cash and card receipts inside the money bag. "I'll take this to the bank in a little while. We need a June party."

He shrugged and sucked back a long drink of the strong brew. "What'd we do last year?"

"June fourteenth. National Bourbon Day."

"Works for me." He put the empty mug in the sink and filled a travel cup for Cammie. "Did you see the shelves in the back storeroom? I think there's a leak in the wall. The paneling looks warped, and some shelves in that back corner are starting to buckle."

I nodded. "Yeah, I saw it. I'll go by Home Depot after the bank and get what we need."

"How 'bout hiring that Patrick fellow or one of his brothers to do the work? We're not destitute, you know. In fact, between the two of us, we've managed to save quite a bit. It would be a great time to...."

Shit, here it comes. Again. "Not yet."

"Sloane, think about it. Expanding into a restaurant makes sense. We have Grandma's recipes, and Cammie can run the kitchen...."

Gordon had raised this idea for years now. The bar had the space to put in a kitchen with a little reconfiguring. It was doable, but Gordon couldn't quite grasp the magnitude of the project. The bar would have to go through a huge remodel, which meant potential lost revenue. Add in the cost of labor, materials, hiring full-time staff, food, equipment, advertising, inspections, and all the other shit needed, it would take a small fortune. We had enough money between us, but this venture had the potential to take every penny and send the needle way into the red. I'd already paid off one massive debt and was saving for something else. I thought he was too.

"The money you've been saving up you told me was earmarked for a house. Cammie's told you time and time again how she feels about living above the bar. She wants a nice place in a family-friendly neighborhood for you two to raise Courtney."

Gordon scoffed and slashed his hand. "Courtney is still a baby, and Cammie said she would love to run her own kitchen someday."

He didn't lie.

Before she got pregnant, Cammie worked as a sous-chef in one of the fancy five-star places in the high-dollar district of the city. "Your daughter won't stay a baby. Children have the tendency to grow. Fast."

"Cammie understands."

"I don't. Gordon, I have one more year to go. Don't fuck with me while I wait."

Gordon made to argue further but gave up. He knew exactly what I referred to even though he forbade me to talk about it out loud. He heaved a gigantic sigh and picked up the travel mug. "I got it, sis. Maybe after next year?"

"We'll see. Now take that bean juice to Cammie before she leaves you."

He grinned. "She loves me too much, and I'm buying her a house someday."

"Still need to put a ring on it."

Gordon ignored my parting shot, and his clomping steps echoed through my loft as he descended.

Chapter Four

"Jameson and a Guinness, please, Sloane."

Patrick eased his aching body on a stool, and Angus did the same. They'd tag-teamed recently on five massive deck jobs with Owen, as well as putting in the fencing and eating area for a dog run at the back of a coffee shop. Connor had not lied to them about business opportunities in the mountain city. They had more jobs lined up for the next few weeks in Black Mountain and Woodfin that meant long hours and huge pay. Rain stalled them last week for two days, but they had caught up by putting up large halogen lights and working past dark.

Sloane worked the bar solo, which was rare for a busy Thursday night. She faced away from them but raised a finger to say she'd heard and would get to them shortly. She finished blending three margaritas and serving them to some women, then pulled two pitchers to fill from the tap.

"Where's Gordon?"

Sloane didn't look up from her task. "Cammie's been sick for a few days, and he had to take care of the baby tonight."

"She gonna be okay?"

"Don't know. She's pretty bad. Gordon's tried to convince her to go to the doctor, but we don't have a great insurance plan." Sloane distractedly pulled the beers. Patrick noticed she didn't execute the perfect pour as she usually did. Normally, she tilted the tulip-shaped glass to form a beautiful foam head and let it settle before topping off. Tonight she jerked down the tap handle and handed them glasses immediately, letting the head froth heavily.

"*You* okay, darlin'?"

She answered with an eye roll and a huff. "I'm fine. Just busy. I called one of the weekend girls to come help, but she's at her other job. She'll come in when she can."

"Yo, sweetheart! We gonna get served sometime this century?"

The call came from a group of businessmen sitting at a table near the back. Sloane lifted two full pitchers in one hand and a tray of glasses in the other. "Be right back."

Patrick winced at the weight she carried in her arms. Ropey with muscle but toothpick thin. He looked around at the other patrons as he shot back his whiskey. The burn traveled down his throat and settled with a comfortable warmth in his stomach. The counter had puddles and debris scattered over its surface, where he'd only seen it meticulously kept. Fuck, she was clearly overwhelmed.

Angus tipped his glass back. "She's having a rough night, eh?"

"Yeah. Those assholes aren't helping much."

Patrick sipped at the beer and watched Sloane grab a few empties from a table and give it a brief swipe. Dammit, the woman was about to work herself to death. He saw her lean on the table as if catching her breath.

"Fuck this shit," he muttered and stepped behind the bar.

Angus grinned at him. "Tryin' to work up some brownie points or helpin' out?"

"Shut up, brother, unless you're gonna come back here and help."

Angus shrugged and joined in.

Sloane came back with a round tray on her hip

and a frown the size of Texas on her face. "What the hell do you think you're doing?"

Patrick pulled a beer from the array of taps for a customer. "Saving your ass, what little of it is there. When was the last time you ate? Christmas?"

She rolled her eyes. "No, smartass. I ate this morning."

He looked at his watch. "It's going on nine o'clock, darlin'."

She waved away his concern. "I'll eat later."

"How 'bout now?"

"I have too much work to do."

A text message ding from her phone interrupted his answer. The utterly defeated look on Sloane's face made him want to hug her. "Shit. Jeanie can't come in after all."

Angus dumped a pile of glasses into the sink with a rattle. "Good thing we're here, eh? We can't mix any fancy drinks, but we can pour beer and bus tables for you. Sit your ass down for a few minutes. You got this, Patrick?"

"I'm on it. Sloane, you like roast beef or turkey?"

She put a load in the dishwasher and closed the door. "You ordering food? You don't have to get me anything."

"I know I don't have to, but I'm going to. What's your choice, or shall I make it for you?"

Thankfully she gave up without further argument. This told Patrick the depth of her fatigue more than the dark circles under her eyes. "Either is fine."

"Cool. McAllister's Deli it is." His fingers danced over his phone and he grinned at her as he ordered. "Grubhub, baby. Best app in the world."

Angus pulled two more beers. "Get us some of those Cinnabon cheesecakes they have. That will put some meat on your bones."

Sloane sat on a stool near the back of the bar area. "I have plenty of meat on me."

Angus laughed. "I think you've been taking those diet pills. Heard of them? No-ass-at-alls?"

Sloane didn't laugh with him. Patrick stopped what he was doing and glanced over. Her eyes were down, and she seemed to be biting her lip. Angus's teasing should have brought out a bit of fire. Instead, she looked... well... hurt.

"Ahh, you gobshite arsehole!" He threw a paper coaster at Angus's head. "Your latest lady love is a yoga teacher. All bendy like a pretzel. I bet she isn't heavy in the ass, either."

Angus caught the coaster and tossed it back. "Sloane knows I'm messing with her." He turned to the seated woman and made a cordial bow. "I sincerely apologize for insulting your delectable ass, madame."

She tried to get huffy, but Angus accomplished his mission, and she laughed out loud. "You two are the biggest clowns I've ever met."

Patrick pulled another three beers and handed her the wad of cash the customer gave him. "Here, love. You can run the register."

The table in the back called for another refill, and Angus carried the pitchers this time.

"They want to know about the karaoke machine. You gonna fire it up?"

Sloane shook her head. "Not tonight. Gordon is the one who knows how to work that thing. Pete helps sometimes, but he's not here."

Patrick took the empty pitchers and loaded them into the washer along with the sink full of glasses. "I can do it. I ran one of these when we had a job in Ocean City."

"No, thanks. Karaoke is for the weekends, and frankly, I'd rather those guys leave as soon as possible. They've been a pain in my ass all night."

"Good point, darlin'. They been giving you a rough time?"

"Nothing I can't handle, but I'm still ready for them to pay up and go."

The food arrived, and Patrick argued with Sloane to go to the tiny back office.

"Stubborn wench. The bar's not gonna implode in the fifteen minutes it'll take for you to eat."

"It's my bar, Patrick MacAteer."

"And it will still be your bar in fifteen minutes. Go."

Her face screwed up at him. "I don't like you very much right now."

He let it slide right off his back. "Oh, darlin', I know you secretly love me. Now go."

She finally left with a growl, and he chuckled at her pique. If her eyes had lasers, he would be ashes by now.

By eleven o'clock, most of the place had emptied. Last call came and went, leaving only a few of the regulars and the loud businessmen. Angus swept the floors while Patrick emptied the dishwasher. Sloane ran the day's reports, then moved to clear and wipe tables.

"Thanks, guys, for helping out. I doubt I could've made it tonight without you. I got it from here if you want to go home."

Patrick stood from his crouched position, and his

back cracked loudly. "No problem, sweetheart. Always glad to help. I don't know about Angus, but you can pay me back in booze or...." He waggled his eyebrows up and down at her.

She barked a laugh at his obvious play. "Booze it is."

"We need two more pitchers over here!" an over-stuffed suit yelled across the room.

"Last call was a half hour ago, buddy. Bar's closed," Sloane called back as she placed a handful of glasses on a tray. A moment later, a hand seized her arm and jerked her around, banging her hip against the table hard enough to move it. Glasses fell and shattered on the floor.

"I said, we need two more pitchers! You deaf?"

Sloane leaned her head back as the man's rancid breath and spittle sprayed in her face. "No, not deaf, asshole. You apparently are. I said last call is over!"

The man's jowly face curled in on itself as he prepared to explode. He didn't get the chance.

Patrick saw red as fury erupted in his head. He rushed over and dropped his arm over the asshole's head, jerking back on his neck and cutting off the shorter man's air. The drunk man was thrown off balance and released Sloane to claw at Patrick's arm, trying to break free. Patrick wanted to squeeze harder. He barely noticed the man's attempts at freeing himself, his rage was that great.

"Patrick, let him go. I'm okay."

He didn't want to. He really didn't, but the pleading expression on Sloane's face had him easing his death grip. His arm dropped, and the man bent over, coughing and choking.

"This is the way it's going to go." Patrick stood tall and spoke loudly and clearly. "You're going to stand up and apologize to the lady. Then you're going to settle your tab and tip her a hundred bucks for the broken glasses and her trouble. Last, you're going to leave peacefully. Anything you don't understand?"

The man's two companions stood up from their table, and Angus moved to stand behind Patrick. Three soft-looking business suits and two tall, strong construction men faced off in the bar.

One side of Patrick's mouth raised. *Not a bad start for a good joke.* "What's it gonna be, boy-o? If you need to fight someone, try me instead of a woman. It's been a while since I had a decent scrap, and I'm not afraid to sit in a jail cell for breaking a jaw." He looked at the other men. "Or two."

The tense moment passed as one of the men pulled out his card and handed it to Sloane. "Sorry for your trouble. Clint's wife took him to the cleaners over the divorce, and..."

"No one here gives a shit. There's no excuse for being an asshole to a woman and putting hands on her. Now get the fuck out," Angus added.

Sloane ran the card and gave it back. The three men left. The jerk who assaulted Sloane had one parting shot. "Service in this place sucks! I'll be posting a bad review!"

Patrick raised a middle finger.

Angus moved to sweep the broken glass. "You all right? That fucker didn't hurt you, did he?"

"I've been through worse."

Patrick still seethed with anger. He'd been in bar fights before and wished like hell one of those men had taken a swing at him. Just one. Then he could have wiped the floor with all of them. How dare he touch Sloane! She had to be less than half his weight and several inches shorter. Fucking son of a bitch. If he ever set foot in this bar again....

"Yo, Patrick. Love you much, brother, but I'd also love to let Sloane close up and get the hell outta here."

Angus's voice penetrated the raging fog, and Patrick inhaled as deeply as he could. He turned to his favorite bartender and almost lost it again when he saw her rub the spot on her arm where that bastard had gripped her. The obvious bruise made him want to chase down the bastard and pound his skull into the wall. "That shit happen a lot?"

Sloane carried the last of the table debris to the big plastic trash can. "Not usually. Had a few incidents recently, but nothing I can't handle."

"What kinds of incidents?"

Sloane leaned over the bar and sighed. "Had a regular who loved to sing during karaoke nights, but sucked at it big time. He made trouble more than once by bothering women who didn't want to be bothered. When he got nasty about it and I had to ban him, he tried to come back and throw his weight around, thinking I'd cave in to his demands because he's a man and I'm a woman, but he forgot who he was talking to. I don't put up with that kind of shit attitude at my bar. Garrett took care of that for me as the guy targeted Bertie for a bit."

Patrick's rage bubbled back up. "Where is he now?"

"Gone. From the bar talk, his mama got her church people to do some sort of intervention thing. A drive-out-the-demons party if you will. Now, he's become a corner preacher raining hellfire and brimstone down off Patterson Street on the other side of town. He hasn't been here in weeks."

"No way could you have handled that guy."

She shrugged and made one last swipe across the bar. "Like I said, I've dealt with worse."

Patrick decided he hated that statement. "Gordon working tomorrow night?"

Sloane tossed the dishtowel into a basket near the office entrance and arched her back with a long groan. "No clue."

Patrick watched her body stretch and thought again about how fragile-looking her thin body appeared. He glanced around the place, thinking about the size of the normal Friday night crowd and the demands they made on weekends. Too much for her to run by herself. "I'll be here."

Chapter Five

I WOULD NEVER IN A MILLION YEARS SAY IT OUT LOUD, but having Patrick help me at the bar turned out to be a godsend in more ways than one. Cammie had more than a passing bug, and we got a crash course in a nasty disease called meningitis. She got sick enough her doctor admitted her to the hospital, and Gordon turned into a full-time Mr. Mom. He did what he could at work; however, his first priority was taking care of his family.

This put me in the position of working bell to bells every day for the past two weeks. I opened. I closed. I did the books. I cleaned. I served. I took inventory. I made up the calendar of events. I posted ads on social media and the website. From the moment my feet hit the floor in the morning to when I could finally go to sleep, I worked. Without Patrick's assistance, I wouldn't have made it.

He showed up every night for a few hours after working a full day himself to pull beers and pour shots. His stamina impressed me, along with his interest in bartending. He learned a few of the more popular mixed drinks, like margaritas, Long Islands, and our own Irish coffee recipe. He'd saved my ass four nights already this week by staying until closing. This would be his second Friday night behind the bar instead of in front of it.

Madhouse described the place tonight. Some conference for a college sorority was in town, and they stuffed my place to capacity. Red and white were their colors, and they were there to drink, party, and hook up. I had Jeannie and Shelley to serve the floor, and Pete, one of my regulars, was nice enough to man the karaoke machine. It was all I could do to keep up.

I mixed up three more pitchers of mojitos and stored them in the back fridge. The ones I made earlier were disappearing like crazy, and it was only seven o'clock. I sent up a prayer for whatever god was on call that night to get someone to start ordering beer when Patrick sauntered in. He launched his hands in the air and made his usual weekend announcement.

"Bow down, mere mortals! Patrick MacAteer is in the hoooooouuuuuuse!"

The out-of-town women had no idea who he was, but they whooped and clapped anyway.

He came behind the bar, and I spared him a brief glance as I fired up the blender for another round of daiquiris.

"Hello, my beautiful Sloane. You can use me anywhere tonight." He waggled his eyebrows and bent to kiss me on the cheek.

My stomach turned over as his lips touched me. His spicy scent wafted over me, and I felt scummy compared to his fresh, clean appearance. He hadn't kissed me before and the sudden heaviness in my gut shook me. I tamped it down firmly. I didn't have time for any distractions, tonight or any night, and frankly, crushing on the new town playboy was a great way to get my heart broken. Not going there.

"Your hair looks great, love." He grinned at me as he washed his hands. "Dark brown or black? Hard to tell, but it's nice."

I had it tied back under a wide blue bandana, hippie style. "Black, like my mood."

"Aw, now, luv. Don't go sour on me. Take a break for a bit while I feed the masses, yeah?"

He turned to face the sea of estrogen surrounding the bar. "Who wants a penis colossus?"

His yell turned the noise volume to a decibel only dogs should be able to hear. I groaned as I poured the daiquiris and added them to a tab. Last week, Patrick found a stash of plastic test tube shot glasses and their serving racks in the back storeroom and came up with the idea of his "signature" drink. The penis colossus was nothing more than a version of a creamsicle shot. Pineapple Jell-O and coconut milk mixed with rum and a squirt of whipped cream on top served in the six-inch tube. It took him minutes to mix his concoction and pour with the stack shaker trick. The whole time he talked and flirted and entertained. The ladies went crazy. What red-blooded heterosexual female wouldn't go a little nuts over getting a "penis colossus" from an enticing man like Patrick?

Still, penis colossus? I supposed I shouldn't complain as the drinks were disappearing and the register kept ringing up sales.

Somewhere around eleven, I slapped down a coaster in front of a new patron without looking to see who it was. "What will it be tonight?"

"Guinness on tap."

Electricity shot down my spine as my brain short-circuited. I froze and raised my gaze to the rich voice I knew so well. One I hadn't heard in years.

Dark brown eyes met mine. His black hair was longer now and hung to his shoulders in waves. Short stubble crossed his upper lip and lower jaw, where he used to shave daily. His Italian heritage showed in his long patrician nose and olive complexion. This face I woke up to daily for three years. This face I kissed at night when the owner moved inside me. This face abandoned me when I'd needed it the most.

Fuck. I forced my mouth into a semi-smile and stuffed my emotions into a remote corner of my mind. "Hello, Claudio. Thought you never drank beer."

His beautiful mouth smiled. "I'm in an Irish pub. I expect the beer is better than the Chianti."

The noise faded a bit as I pulled the Guinness and waited for the settle. I could hear Patrick amusing the crowd by singing Def Leppard's "Pour Some Sugar on Me" along with the women who were up on the stage. Out of the corner of my eye, I could see him gyrating as he mixed his shots. He turned and twerked his butt at the women at the bar. Total chaos, but he loved every minute. He raised his green eyes from his bent-over position, gave me his best what-can-I-do smile, and winked. I rolled mine back at him. *Cliché much?*

"The new guy looks happy."

I finished the pour and set the glass in front of him, willing my hands to be steady. "How do you know he's new?"

He took a sip of the beer head and licked the foam that decorated his lips. "I moved back a few weeks ago and found him and his brother renovating the deck at my parents' place. I overheard him say something about how much he liked helping out a cute bartender at his favorite Irish pub. It didn't take long for me to figure out which one and who he talked about. You look good, Sloane."

A spring inside my chest ratcheted tighter at his words. *"You look good, Sloane."*

They were just words. They meant nothing. My heart jumped anyway at the crumb. *Wait, Patrick called me cute? The same man that badgered me into eating almost every night?* "You look good too. Nice beard."

A lopsided smile broke across his face at my return compliment. Questions crowded my head, and I didn't know what to ask.

Still a freelance photographer? Gallery shows now or still working the wedding circuit? Feel like shit because of what you did to me?

Patrick rescued me again without knowing it. He came up behind him, slung an arm around my shoulders, and pulled me in close. "Hey, it's my buddy Clyde! How's it hanging?"

Claudio's smile collapsed a little, and he sat up straighter. "It's Claudio."

"Cool." He yelled behind him with his other arm overhead and pointing at my ex, "Hey, Rachel and Marnie, come meet my pal, Claudio. He's drinking by himself and could use some company."

Two giggling women came over. "It's Jill and Gloria, silly!"

Patrick grinned and put a hand over his heart. "I'm so sorry, my beauties. I got so dazzled when you spoke to me, I lost all brain function."

His over-acting choked me a little and I covered it up with a cough. *Seriously, do women really fall for that shit?* Apparently they did as the duo tittered and cuddled up on either side of a miffed-looking Claudio.

"Sloane, I need four Singapore slings and an old fashioned. We're getting low on rum. I'm gonna run to the back to reload. Can you handle this for a minute?" he whispered in my ear.

That was all I needed to snap back into work mode. "Yeah, and grab a couple of vodkas too while you're at it. Please and thank you."

He smacked a quick kiss on my forehead, and I stiffened as he lifted the bar leaf. *It's nothing, Sloane. Don't insert your head into your ass over this man.*

By the time I made last call, I was ready to drop. The red and white female brigade had consumed more than their fair share of booze and had moved on to whatever activities awaited them for the rest of the night. A few of my regulars stayed after to enjoy a few quiet minutes without the blare of the karaoke machine. Jeannie and Shelley helped clean up the floor before they left, but the majority still fell on my shoulder. Patrick leaned over the bar, talking with a superbly drunk woman while I ran the last load of glasses in the washer. I didn't see Claudio leave or if he had dual company. The place emptied to the point where it was only me, Patrick, and the one drunk woman. I finished wiping down when I saw him walking out the front door. His arm sat cozily around her waist, and her hand palmed his butt.

A sting smacked me between the eyes like a dart from the games in the back of the room. I had no reason or no expectations for anything else, but I still had the urge to cry. Exhaustion could be part of the reason, but I knew it wasn't the only factor.

Alone. I was alone and the weight of the silent bar crushed into me. The crowd of women had left either to go back to the hotel with roommates and friends or temporary hookups. Most of my regulars had gone home to be with partners or spouses. I imagined Claudio slept somewhere sandwiched between the two women Patrick sicced on him. Now he had found a willing partner for the night and left me by myself, without a backward glance.

It hurt. I didn't know why and it shouldn't have, but it did.

I tossed my towel into the laundry basket and pulled out the push broom. As tired as I was, I needed to finish sweeping up before falling into bed. Some people found it amazing at what the human body was capable of enduring. I found it amazing that we had to endure it in the first place. Physical tolls could drive a person to the point of becoming a health hazard, whereas the mental tolls made it much worse.

No matter. I had a job to do and a bar to keep up. Instead of wallowing in a "poor me" attitude, I mentally listed the good stuff in my life.

I had a brother who loved me.

I had a precious little niece who grinned every time she saw me.

I had friends.

I had a successful business.

I had a decent place to live.

I had my life.

I was so lost in my thoughts that I jumped when the broom was pulled from my hands. Patrick had returned.

"Oy, darlin', you really need to slow down. I'll finish this up."

"What happened to your... uh... date? I thought you'd gone for the night."

He looked perplexed. "What's her name? Way too hammered to get back to her hotel by herself. I put her in an Uber and tipped the driver to make sure she got in the building."

"Oh."

He smirked at me as he brushed a pile into the dustpan. "You thought I'd try to hit that, didn't you?"

A blush heated up my cheeks. "Yeah, well, it's not like you haven't tried with three out of the four single females that walk in the door. I guess I made a wrong assumption."

Patrick dumped the full dustpan and leaned on

the broom handle. "If she'd been more sober, then yeah, I might have tried, but she was too wasted to make that call. I like sex. Uncomplicated and uncommitted, but fucking a woman who can't even form a coherent thought? It's not right."

He put the broom and dustpan back in its customary spot and gazed at me with an intensity I didn't expect. "Do you really think I'm that much of a bastard?"

I swallowed the big lump of crow pie that lodged in my throat. "I'm sorry, Patrick. I shouldn't have gone there. You've been such a big help to me. I had no right to make that judgment call."

He stared a moment more, then grinned. He held his hands in front of his chest as if cupping two large melons. "She did have some nice big knockers, eh? Maybe if she would do all the work...."

I laughed and shook my head, not wanting to show any other reaction. Inside, something died. "You are such a horn dog."

"Hello, Pot, I'm Kettle. Don't try to deny it, love. I saw you teasing a man or two tonight. Calvin kept his eyes on you even with Rona sticking her tongue in his ear."

"It's Claudio, and I could have died happy

without that visual. I know him from a long time ago. We... we used to date."

Patrick stopped and his face grew mildly serious. "Is he tryin' to start up again?"

"I don't know, but it's not happening. I have too much on my plate to consider it or anything else."

He dropped his eyes back to his task, and I swore I heard him mutter, "Good."

Chapter Six

Patrick pulled his truck into one of the reserved spots in the alley at the back of the building. Sloane's ancient Corolla and Gordon's Honda minivan sat side by side, leaving just enough room for him to park there. It was nice not to have to search for a place on the street or wrestle his large vehicle in a miniscule parking deck spot.

The noise from the pub bled out onto the sidewalk as he entered. May celebrated two bar parties back-to-back. *Star Wars* Day on the fourth and Cinco de Mayo on the fifth. Both happened on a Monday and Tuesday respectively, and people packed the place both nights it seemed from the volume.

He spotted Sloane behind the bar, smiling, mixing, and serving. He liked watching her work.

Her hands were in constant motion keeping up with orders. Small bartender tricks like pop-and-catch for bottle tops, shallow spins of glasses around her thumb, and bumping an empty off her elbow into the recycle bin. He'd love to learn how to do more of that shit. A sheen of sweat covered her face, and tonight her hair color was stripes of bright pink, yellow, and green. Last night it had been chocolate brown and styled like the latest female *Star Wars* character, Rae.

Colored tips, full dye jobs, up-dos, braids, she kept him guessing as to what her hair would look like from night to night. Her clothes were always the same. Black T-shirt with the business logo across the front, torn sleeveless at the shoulders, faded jeans, and sneakers. Her physique showed cut muscles on a tiny body. He sighed. *I bet she didn't eat tonight. Again.*

Gordon also worked the bar tonight. Cammie was home from the hospital, and since then, he tried to help out for part of the night when able. He still had to watch after his baby girl while Cammie was on the mend, she was still very weak and tired easily.

Fatigue hit Patrick as well. Last week he'd put in some seriously long hours working during the day. Up around six thirty to get to the job sites by seven, then knocking off around five to grab food and a shower before heading to Gallaghers's. It had become a regular thing for him, and he liked it a lot, even when he got bone-ass tired.

Since helping out, Sloane insisted on paying him something, even though he'd told her he didn't want it. They settled on a share of the tip jar. Truth was, he enjoyed being behind the bar instead of in front of it. He had learned a bunch of popular mixed drinks already and seriously contemplated going to bartender school. The parties and promotions, local brews, and the outgoing social atmosphere of the place suited him, almost better than construction. He still liked working with his brothers, especially since the money was outstanding, but he loved the pub atmosphere. Every time he walked into the bar, he got a second wind.

"Bow down, mere mortals! Patrick is in the hoooooooouuuuuuuse!"

A deafening wave of yells and whoops greeted his ears. People knew him and some even came here just to see him work. A fan club of women already waited for him. He kissed them all with quick, dry pecks before slipping behind the bar. Tonight in celebration of the holiday, the featured drinks were margaritas in every kind of flavor. Lime, lemon, raspberry, coconut, pineapple, blue curacao, and for some reason, watermelon. Patrick shuddered at the thought, but Sloane claimed they were popular enough to include on the menu. Tequila sunrise also sat on the drink specials' chalkboard, and of course, shots of Jose Cuervo.

"Hey, Patrick!" A blonde with hair teased out beyond normal capacity pouted suggestively at him. "You missed me?"

She'd been on the prowl there before with her posse of decked-out ladies. Tonight was no different.

"Just saving the best for last, darlin'," he said with a wink. *Adelaide, Abigail, Alanna, something like that. I think.* He leaned across the bar with the intent of a quick peck like the others, but Alesha-Aleena-Alexa had other plans. She grabbed his chin with her long red talons and held him in place while she laid a big one on him. Her tongue pushed at his lips, and he let her in for a sweep. *Well, if that's what she wanted.* He slanted and took over deepening the kiss. His tongue pushed hers away and thrust into her mouth, mimicking the act of penetration. She groaned at his dominance and let him plunder her thoroughly. He ended the kiss to catcalls and whoops from the on-looking patrons. Allyson-Alexandra-Amelia sat back and panted. Her face flushed with heat and her eyes glazed.

Patrick grinned and smacked his lips. "Raspberry. Want another one, love?"

The woman nodded, still dazed.

He winked again. "Coming right up." He turned away from the group as one of them said, "Oh my God, Reese, that was soooo hot!"

Reese, eh? Damn, he needed to get better with names.

Sloane moved over and let him get to the mixing. He noticed her jaw flexing in irritation but didn't know what caused it. "Something wrong?"

Sloane tossed a cherry into a Tequila Sunrise before answering. "Just surprised to see Reese so soon after her surgery. Last time she came in here, she had B cups. Those puppies are at least double Ds now."

He raised his eyebrows and pursed his lips. "Double Ds, eh? Not that I don't love a big rack to burrow into at night, but fake ones aren't my favorite. Nice to look at but they don't move right. Give me natural over size and I'm a happy man. Take you, for example."

She stiffened next to him. "What the hell?"

He noticed her anger and spoke in his most soothing voice. "Now, Sloane, my precious, I'm not trying to be a dick, but I've got eyes. I know you've not been under the knife for a boob job, and I bet you're not planning on it anytime soon. I'm just saying that if you were in my bed, I'd be just as happy with small or large as long as they're real."

Her eyes shimmered for a moment before a sharp bark of laughter came out. "As if that would ever happen."

She turned to serve the drink and make a note on a tab. Patrick noticed her hands shook but let it go as Garrett, Bertie, and Rhyleigh showed up.

He beamed at them. "How's it hangin', brother? Bertie, my secret love, when will you leave this loser's ass and come with me?"

"Maybe after he finishes building my new garden shed." She accepted his cheek kiss and miraculously found an empty stool.

"How 'bout you, Rhyleigh? He grinned, proud of himself for getting her name right. "Wanna walk on the wild side?"

The tiny yoga instructor blushed. "Um... no, thank you. Have you seen Angus?"

"Not since we quit work for the day. He left the house before I did. Don't have a clue where he went."

Her face fell, and Patrick felt sorry for the girl.

She obviously had a crush on his twin, and he had thought Angus might be in the same frame of mind. They had rented a small month-to-month two-bedroom house while staying in Asheville long term. For years, they had partied together, but Angus had started going out alone and not saying where or what he was doing. Patrick spent more time at the bar and rarely noticed his brother's comings and goings. He knew Angus hadn't brought any women back to the house, so there was that, but he went out early and came home late several times a week. Patrick assumed he was doing Rhyleigh, but perhaps not.

"Watermelon margaritas? Those are either fantastic or terrible. Make me one when you get the chance, please?" Bertie trilled, bringing him back.

He chuckled and flipped a coaster off his knuckles to place in front of her. "Your wish is my command, my queen."

The night wore on with more drinks, more laughter, more singing from the karaoke stage, and lots of fun. Gordon left at ten to go be with his family, leaving only Sloane and Patrick to run the bar. Garrett, Bertie, and Rhyleigh left a few minutes after.

Reese led his nightly harem of women and kept

up her plays. She sat teasing the straw with her tongue and hunching her shoulders to draw his attention to her ample cleavage anytime he brought her a new drink. Another woman made a point of stroking his hand anytime he handed her a glass. The air got heavier when Reese and three of her posse got up to do Niki Minaj's "Anaconda" on the karaoke stage. They more or less shrieked the rap lyrics to the avid onlookers, but the crowd lost it completely when they turned around, squatted, and twerked in tandem rhythm.

Patrick watched the row of shimmying butts and let out a huge whoop. "Twerk off!" he yelled at the top of his lungs and climbed on top of the bar. The entire place shifted their attention to him as he lifted a shot to his mouth and threw it back. Then he turned around, bent over, and proceeded to pump his ass in the air. The noise rose to deafening. *Fuck, he loved it here.* It was a place he felt truly at home. A place where he belonged and fit in like the perfect mitered piece. He was... he was... fuck... he was so goddamn happy it made him high.

His eyes rose from his bent position to meet Sloane's scowling face. Any other time, he might be taken aback at her anger. She'd been prickly all night, and he had no idea the cause of it. Just behind her, he spotted Claudio with a fresh beer in front of him. The man took a drink and grimaced at the taste. If beer wasn't his thing, why was he here? Only one reason. Sloane.

Maybe it was the excitement of the big party atmosphere. Maybe he was too hyped up from adrenaline. Maybe it was the sudden surge of jealousy at Claudio's focused attention on Sloane. Whatever it was, he gave into it. To the screams and hollers of the people and the shot of liquid encouragement, he hopped down off the bar and grabbed Sloane and pulled her off her feet against his body.

"What the fu—" she started, and he ended it with his mouth on hers.

He never expected it to happen.

Lightning struck from his spine to his knees and he nearly dropped her. The noise faded as his entire being concentrated only on the woman in his arms. His tongue speared into her mouth and he tasted mint. Altoids. He remembered her habit of chewing them to keep her breath fresh when she spoke to customers. His brain registered the sharp flavor as it shut down and the blood from his head pooled into his groin. His dick shot up and pulsed behind his jeans zipper and the heart in his chest beat overtime. Christ, he had wanted to do this for so fucking long.

The second strike hit him harder.

She kissed him back.

Her stiff body relaxed, and her arms came up around his shoulders to anchor herself there. He sensed rather than heard the moan from her throat and a maelstrom of desire flamed in his gut. Never had he experienced this kind of reaction to a woman. It was addictive, and he wanted more. Her head slanted and their tongues dueled to see who dominated. Her heady taste filled him to the brim, and he wished he could bury himself inside her and stay.

He let her slide to her feet, and she arched to keep as close to him as possible, sucking and licking at his lips, until he felt like he would burst. The whoops, catcalls, and whistles kept going. *Fuck, these people have to go,* Patrick thought as he raised a hand with the intent of running it through Sloane's colorful hair. *I have a woman I need to take care of.* My *woman.*

She jerked away, breathing heavily and putting some distance between them. In one heartbeat Patrick saw passion and desire reflected back. The promise of something extraordinary. The next heartbeat, she shut it down with a resounding crash.

Her hand whipped out and cracked across his

cheek to the roaring laughter of the observing crowd.

"Ho no! You got owned!"

"Crash and burn!"

"Don't fuck where you eat!"

For a moment, Patrick had unfamiliar emotions hit him. Disbelief, denial, embarrassment, and above all, pain. Not the physical pain of his stinging cheek. Pain in his heart from Sloane's rejection. Never in his life had this happened to him. Women loved him. Young, old, big, small, it didn't matter, and they surrounded him in droves. His entire life had been one big smorgasbord of women ever since he lost his virginity. He never had a girlfriend or any kind of serious relationship. He didn't have to—his roaming lifestyle didn't work for long-term commitments—and he hadn't met a woman yet that he wanted for something more.

Until Sloane.

He straightened and met the eyes of the woman who occupied his thoughts. Unshed tears shimmered in her eyes. Her lips quivered, and she shook like she was coming apart and the only thing holding her together was her arms wrapped around her middle. Patrick saw the war taking place inside her. Anger, confusion, and sadness raced over her face, one after the other. Patrick didn't know what to expect. She could have thrown him out. She could have screamed and cursed him. She could have flown into his arms for round two, three, and four. Instead, she did the last thing he expected.

She fled.

Straight past the bar to the back office.

She left him alone in a bar full of people laughing hysterically at the show. He swallowed the lump in his throat and turned to face the music. He put aside the maelstrom of emotions swirling in his head and did what he did best. His mouth spread in the biggest smile he could fake, and he made a courtly bow to the amusement of the screaming masses.

"Put some AC/DC on that machine, Pete! Let's rock this hoooouuuuuuse!" He raised his arms with pointed horn hands to the ceiling.

Pete had a solemn expression on his face but nodded and complied. "Thunderstruck" poured from the speakers and the entire bar sang along.

"Jesus, we're gonna need to start wearing earplugs or be deaf by fifty." Gordon sidled up to Patrick. His hair was sticking up in a few places and his clothes were wrinkled. "Sloane woke me up and told me she got sick to her stomach. I'm supposed to finish out the night. She said she needed to take a rest. Sam over there said something different. Which one is right?"

Patrick pulled a beer and handed it to a customer. He recognized the protective brother mode and didn't blame Gordon for it. More than once as kids, he and his brothers had scrapped with other boys that bothered Eva, their only sister. Sure, he had picked on her and played pranks on her until one of them turned dangerous, but when it came down to brass tacks, he'd mess up anyone who tried to fuck with her. "Both. If he's saying I kissed Sloane, yeah, I did. She's not happy about it, but I'm not sorry either."

Patrick fully expected Gordon to take a swing at him, adding a broken nose and bloody lips to the meager damage Sloane gave him. Another shock hit him as a huge grin broke out over Gordon's face. "It's about damn time. By the way, what the fuck is that asshole Claudio doin' here?"

Patrick glanced over at the seated man. A short blonde woman had pulled him into a conversation, even though his body language said he wanted to be alone. "Been in a couple times. I think he comes in just to talk to Sloane. Orders beer he never finishes and stares at her like she's a cake and he wants a slice. Annoying as shit, but she told me they used to be tight."

Mild-mannered Gordon sneered as he pulled a beer from the tap. "Not just tight. They were engaged. Fucker dropped her like a hot skillet when—"

"When what?"

"When life sent... challenges. If someone can't stick around when the goin' gets tough, they don't need to come sniffin' around when things are good. She's not thinkin' 'bout takin' him back, is she?"

The unfamiliar green-eyed monster tapped Patrick on the shoulder again. "I don't think so." *She better fucking not!*

He faced the bar to take an order. "What'll it be, man?"

Patrick faked his exuberance until he thought he'd puke. By the time the bar emptied, he was totally drained and ready to melt into the floor. Gordon and the waitresses did the majority of the cleanup while Patrick took stock.

"Sloane will come down tomorrow morning and run the reports off the register. She's the one who knows how it works." Gordon finished sweeping and put the broom and dustpan back in its place. "I don't know what we would've done if you hadn't stuck around and helped us these past weeks. I owe you for that."

Patrick stood up from where he crouched in front of the cooler. "It's no trouble at all. I like being here. A lot." He looked around the bar. "I fit in. The people, the party, the music, all of it makes me feel like I belong here. I don't remember ever being a part of something like I am here. Weird, isn't it?"

Gordon reflected. "Not really. I believe we all have places in life where we belong and people we're supposed to be with. It's rare to find them. Every day, you see people on the streets or the internet searchin' for somethin', somewhere to be, or someone to be with. There's people who end up settlin' for less and end up gettin' mad and bitter about it. Others spend a lifetime searchin' and never findin'. It's the lucky ones that click into that happy place wherever it happens to be."

Patrick chuffed and grinned. "Fuckin' philosopher as well as bartender, eh? What if you've had a good life even if you hadn't found that special place?"

"I said happy, not good. You can make good money, drive a cool car, have a nice house, pretty wife and kids, and still not be happy. Think about all them rich dudes out there who have all that shit and cheat on their spouses all the time. Hell, you met Maggie, the cougar. If she and Sean were happy, they'd do everything in their power not to fuck it up."

Patrick emptied and started counting the tip jar. The agreement was that waitresses could keep all the personal tips from serving the floor and they would divide the jar tips amongst the working bartenders. He liked his carefree life, but was he happy? He always thought so until lately. Connor had found his other half in Beverly and being stepfather to four brilliant kids. Anyone who saw them said they belonged with each other. Melanie and Owen, two opposite people who should have never got together, fit like perfect puzzle pieces and had their own growing family of children. Patrick contemplated Garrett's past situation with the bitch from hell who sucked the life from his brother and how his woman, Bernadette, had filled him back up again. They'd found their places. Happy places with women who loved and supported them while Patrick still played and drank and fucked. He liked to play and drink and fuck, but did that make him happy? Truly happy?

One of the twenty-dollar bills caught his eye with some red coloring. A big lipstick kiss smeared across

Andrew Jackson's face along with a note penned in the corner.

Call me, baby, and I'll give you more than a kiss.

Shit, what was her name again? Began with an R? He'd gotten notes like this before, scrawled on napkins or the backs of receipts. He'd be lying if he said he didn't take up a few of those offers, but if he admitted it to himself, the encounters were stale. The woman got off, and he got off, but that was all. The one-night sex marathons he'd done for years had become dull and unsatisfying. He hadn't been with a woman since just before he'd started at the bar, and counting back, realized he didn't miss it much.

The biggest joy in his life was coming and working at the pub and seeing Sloane. *Christ, I hope I didn't fuck that up.*

That thought followed with another. *Which do I want? The pub or the woman? One more than the other? Fuck!*

He placed the lipstick-coated bill in his pile to hide it and called to Gordon, "I got you and Sloane's cash over here. Nice haul tonight."

"Glad to hear it. You heading out?"

No, I'm heading up to Sloane's apartment. I need to

see her. Would she open the door? Probably not tonight.
"Yeah, I'm done."

"You gonna be back tomorrow?"

"If Sloane will let me back in, yeah."

Gordon nodded. "She will. Remind me to show you the shelves in the storeroom."

"I already saw them. I don't have a day I can schedule until the week after next, but I'll put it on the calendar for me and Angus. Cool?"

"Cool."

Patrick left to let Gordon finish locking up. He opened the door to his truck and craned his neck backwards to look at the top floor of the building. A light shone in the third-floor window and another one on the roof. Patrick clenched his jaw. *Please, God, don't let me have fucked this up.*

Please don't let me have fucked this up!

My hands shook as I stood on my deck and stared out into the sea of city lights. I took another hit off the cigarette and roughly coughed at the caustic smoke filling my lungs. If Gordon came up and caught me, he'd have an absolute conniption. I wouldn't blame him as I hadn't had a cigarette in over four years, and the pack I pulled this one from was at least that old.

Fuck, why did I do that? I stubbed the white stick that was left and took a long drink of water. I thought about bringing a bottle of booze up here, but I didn't want to go down that route. Drinking myself into oblivion had happened more than once in my life, but it was not a habit I wanted to repeat if I could help it. Both times, I'd felt like shit the day after and neither time had solved my problem.

Patrick kissed me.

I could still feel the imprint of his mouth on mine, his tongue demanding entry, his taste, the texture of his lips, the masterful way he molded mine to fit. I shuddered and my belly soared on wings of fire at the memory.

Fuck, get it together, Sloane!

Yes, Patrick MacAteer was a handsome man and had such a charismatic aura around him that people were drawn in. The good looks, fun attitude, and devil-may-care-bad-boy vibe appealed to lots of women, but I should have been immune to all of that. Apparently I wasn't.

I was very aware that Patrick didn't ascribe to the one-woman man idea. If the bar talk had any merit, he'd had several hookups in the past couple months, and I vowed a long time ago I would not be another notch on someone's bedpost. Not again. Still, every night when he made his grand entry, I got warm fuzzies that he was here. I loved his smiles as I showed him a new drink recipe, and his enthusiasm in being behind the bar with me. I'd made up my mind that I could be satisfied with those few pieces of him that were mine that I didn't have to share, but after he kissed me tonight, would that be enough?

Fuck, fuck, fuck! Tears filled my eyes and spilled over my cheeks. I gave up trying to keep them in since no one was around to see me.

Chapter Seven

PATRICK SHOWED UP AT THE BAR AROUND LUNCH TIME the next day.

"Sloane?"

The voice I didn't really want to hear came from the back entrance where we parked our cars. I'd given Patrick the code so he could take out the trash and not get stuck outside. He'd have to walk the length of the alley to get back to the bar. Now I regretted that decision as he walked in from the office to where I sat.

I'd run the reports from last night and instead of going back up to my empty apartment, I decided to stay in the empty bar and take care of the paperwork. My back stiffened, and I looked at the man who occupied my dreams. He wore works jeans—

white with age and stained with paint. His T-shirt had seen better days as well and sported small tears and more stains. He had twisted his long hair in a braid and pulled it back in a Viking man-bun. He looked hot and not due to the sheen of sweat covering him from the budding summer heat. God, did I have to do this? I was so not ready to face him.

"Hi, Patrick. I... um... didn't expect you."

He set a white bag on the counter from a local sandwich shop. "I know. I'm on a lunch break and figured I'd come see you. Apologize and clear the air."

"Apologize?"

His green eyes looked dull as he took a stool close to me and sat down. "Things got out of hand last night and I went overboard. I should not have grabbed you like that and I'm sorry."

Of all the possibilities, this one I expected the least. I stayed silent while he continued to talk.

"You have every right to ban my ass, and if you do, I'll understand. I hope you won't, though. I can't tell you why, but at the end of a workday, no matter if it's a good day or a shit one, I look forward to being here. I love walking in and hearing people call my name. I love hearing the karaoke shit. I get a real kick out of mixing drinks for people and striving for the perfect Guinness pour."

I could have been a raging bitch and told his ass off, but it would be fake. The truth was every night when he showed up, a little thrill ran through me when he announced his booming entry. If he had any inkling of that, he'd probably run for the hills. I'd end up crumpled into a fetal ball and cry over lost crushes. Ignoring the problem meant it wasn't really there, right?

Life still had only one direction. Forward. And I had to keep moving. I snatched open the bag and pulled out a paper-wrapped sandwich. "I don't do pickle spears. It's yours if you want it."

His face split into a shit-eating grin.

"Oh, yes, love. I want it."

Chapter Eight

PATRICK CAME IN NIGHTLY SINCE "THE NIGHT OF THE kiss" and his follow-up day visit. His behavior seemed subdued, but damned if he didn't pay more attention to me. He often called in dinner orders and badgered me until I went into the office to eat. He made sure he did the heavy lifting. "Gotta keep up my pretty figure, sweetheart." Then he'd flex his rounded bicep and his harem sighed.

Yeah, I did too a little.

Gordon thought it was hilarious that he made a big deal of hovering around me when Claudio appeared. I tripped over him twice one night and yelled at him to find both feet or get out of my way. Instead, he put that panty-melting grin on his face and swept me up to dance with him. "We should do a *Dancing with the Stars* kinda thing here sometime. People would love it!"

I gave in and danced with him to the amusement of my bar people.

This afternoon, I sat in the office and listen to Patrick and Angus as they worked to pull down the rotten shelves and put in new ones. It was amazing to see how they worked together in the small space.

"Third shelf mount needs to come down about two inches. Got an outlet back here and don't need to block it."

"Head space still good with a two-inch relief?"

"Yep. Looks good. Mark it and cut."

I didn't understand half of what they said, but the shelves they designed were stronger and sturdier than the last crude set, and also made better use of the space. I could see why they had so many jobs lined up. If all the MacAteer brothers worked this well together, I put money down they'd have a castle complete with turrets and a moat built in a week or two.

Gordon and Cammie came down with little Courtney. They were taking a trip over to the Botanical Gardens near the university campus. The baby's light blonde curls she got from her Mom, but her bright blue eyes were all Gordon. She chortled with glee when she spotted me.

"Headin' out for a while, sis. Bring back food?"

"No thanks. I'll get something later. I need to finish the paperwork before the accountant gets here."

"Jeez, that's today?"

"Yep. Leave the front door open for her, will ya?"

"Sure thing. Be back in a couple of hours."

I nodded and waved a hand over my head as I clicked away with the mouse. The recent uptick in tourism showed in the profits, while expenses remained level. This was good news and perhaps it was time to think about Gordon's idea of opening a restaurant along with the pub. For the longest time, I'd nixed the idea as I didn't want to gamble on what we'd built already, but I'd been thinking about it more and more. If anything, I'd learned life had no guarantees and sometimes you had to roll the dice and take a chance. Maybe it was time. I scratched a few numbers down in speculation. If we took out a business loan against the building instead of using all our savings, we could possibly make it happen. It would triple my workload of course, as Gordon didn't care about the intricacies of stocking toilet paper, regular health inspections, and alcohol permits, but this was his pet project. One he's been wanting to start for years and I knew once he committed himself, he'd work hard to make it succeed. Taking out a loan could be risky, but Gordon wanted this expansion badly. He and Cammie, both had stood behind me when I needed them both. It was time for me to return that support.

I sat back in the booth and took a big swig of the diet soda I shot from the soda gun. A piece of ice cube slipped into my mouth and I crunched it while thinking. What if, instead of reconfiguring the bottom floor space, we made the second floor into the restaurant? The open space was bigger than my apartment so plenty of room existed already. Construction could happen and the bar not have to close at all which meant profits should stay steady. Cammie had put in a top-notch kitchen closer to what she used at her work. They really wanted to move and get settled somewhere before Courtney started kindergarten. Once that timeline got figured out, maybe it wouldn't take too much to get the space ready.

The muted screech of a wood saw pierced my daytime speculations. Patrick and his brothers knew plenty about building and renovating. Hell, the family business had been called Irish Pub Builders when their father ran it. Patrick would give me honest answers and fair pricing if Gordon and I decided to pull the trigger on this new business venture. The more I thought about it, the more I liked the idea.

Gallaghers's Bar and Grill. Gallaghers's Pub and Grill. Gallaghers's Irish Pub and Restaurant.

I scribbled some names in the margin of a legal pad I kept in case the accountant needed paper. My attention was so engrossed that a voice right behind me sent me three feet in the air and threw my heart into arrhythmia.

"Hey, Sloane. Didn't mean to scare you. The door was open, so I thought I'd come in and see you with no one else around to interrupt."

Claudio slid into the booth opposite me and moved my computer to the side leaving no barrier between us. I picked up my drink to cover my shock and get my nerves calmed. "What are you doing here?"

He gave a familiar one-sided shrug and leaned over his forearms on the table. "Had a gig just down the street. Pictures to make ad copy for a coffee shop that has a new dog run in the back. Really cool place. We should go sometime. I remember you loved your coffee in the morning."

That word knife slid between my ribs with perfect precision. Unexpected pain blossomed in my chest as I recalled how he used to make me coffee and bring it to me in bed every morning. More often than not, he tumbled me back into the sheets and made love to me. So much time had passed that it surprised me how much the memory hurt. "I don't drink as much coffee as I used to."

"Oh. Is that because of—"

"No, I just don't drink that much coffee anymore."

"Okay." His eyes couldn't meet mine for very long. They darted around the room, taking in the furnishings as if he'd never seen them before. "Business going good?"

"Yes." I knew my short, clipped answers were rude and my mom would have popped the back of my head already if she were here to listen to me. I couldn't help it. It bugged the snot out of me that I still found Claudio to be attractive, but my trust in him had been so shattered, I couldn't stand to look at him. "I'm not clear why you're here. It's not to ask me out as that time has long gone and I'm sure it's not to check on how well the pub is doing."

He cleared his throat. "I came to apologize about

how things ended between us. It's been eating me alive ever since I moved back to town."

"How things ended between us? You texted me as you were on your way out of town for that cruise ship gig."

"Yes, I did. It was a dick move to make."

"Michelle, my maid of honor, took off with you. Still together?"

He wrinkled his nose and scratched the tip with one finger. I recognized his tell for when he got irritated. "We went our separate ways last year. She stayed with the ships and I came home."

And moved back in with your parents 'cause you had nowhere else to go. "I do not see why that bothers you now instead of four years ago."

"Look, Sloane I was having a rough time too, and—"

My temper flared. "Rough time? *You* were having a rough time? I was at the lowest point of my fucking life and you left me. Now you want to apologize to make yourself feel better? I don't know what you're trying to accomplish, but I don't want any part of it."

"Sloane—"

A white bag suddenly plunked down on the table, next to the pile of papers. "Move those will ya, sweetheart? Angus ran out and brought us burgers from that farm place a few streets over. Don't want to get grease all over them."

He whipped his dusty T-shirt over his head. "Damn, it's hotter than Satan's toenails back there. First chance I get, I'm gonna check the ductwork. Something's not right about it. Scooch over, love."

My mouth dried up at the sight of Patrick's sweaty chest and perfect delineated abs. His physique didn't come from the gym, but his daily construction workout. A smattering of hair decorated his round pecs, and small gold bars pierced both nipples. I could see the tattoo of a green bowler hat just below his flat navel. A tattoo? I wondered what the rest of it looked like.

He plopped down next to me and took a big swallow of my diet soda before opening the bag. "Got your favorite one with the egg on top and sweet potato fries. Angus is in the back cleaning up and will be here in a bit."

Patrick's position placed his arm and leg tight against my side and I believed it was deliberate because of the other man's presence. "Hey, Clarence. Long time, man. Sorry, I didn't know you were here, or I'd have ordered something for you. Mind if we eat in front of you?"

"Claudio" came the tight-lipped reply. He wrinkled his nose and scratched the tip again.

Patrick slapped a hand to his forehead. "Right, right, I'm sorry. I'm really bad with names."

He unloaded the bag and Angus came from behind the bar with several water bottles in his hands. "Shelves are done, but there's a spot on the floor close to the walk-in that's buckling a bit. Best get it fixed before it goes through to the sub-flooring. Next week good for that?"

Patrick took a huge bite of his burger. "Owen said the Carr job will take till Thursday. Friday's open. That good for you, baby?"

"Um... yeah."

"Cool. We'll get it on the calendar. What 'cha got there, love?" He pressed in closer and slung his free arm around my shoulders.

The sudden move flustered me, and I cleared my throat before answering, "Just some sketches about a possible project. Gordon's been wanting to explore opening a restaurant to go with the pub, and I'm thinking about where to put it. Like what it would take for the second floor of the building to be converted."

He bit into a potato wedge and held it up to feed me the rest. "Eat, baby."

Baby? I opened my mouth and ate from Patrick's hand. Who knows why I did it? Maybe just to fuck with Claudio. He scratched his nose again.

Patrick poked at the drawing, pointedly ignoring the fuming man across from us. "Have to look up the regs for fire safety shit. Probably need different outlets with grounding breakers. Plumbing good for bathrooms?"

"I don't know."

Angus answered, "We'll go up and take a quick look if that's okay with Gordon."

Apparently both brothers were of the same mind to ignore the third man at the table. Claudio rose to leave. "Sorry to bother you, Sloane. We'll finish this conversation another time."

Patrick answered back, "Yeah, sorry, man, but you know how it is. We're gonna be pretty busy later. Lots to do. See you soon, yeah?"

Why did I feel like a toy between two toddlers?

Claudio scratched his nose. "I got it." He stiffly walked out the door.

Patrick pushed a cardboard box towards me, popped the top and stole a sweet potato fry. "Get started on that, sweetheart. Angus and I have one more job this afternoon and we need time to take some measurements."

"What just happened?"

He looked at me with the most innocent expression he could muster. "We brought food, 'cause I bet you haven't eaten decent today, and we're gonna look at your space upstairs. Did I miss something?"

I sighed and let it go. The burger smelled great and tasted even better. "Not really."

"That guy bother you?"

"No. Not for a long time."

Patrick looked at my face for a long moment. "Good. Now what kind of floor is in the apartment?"

"You cut this one a half inch too short, boy-o. You okay?"

Patrick stopped hammering a framing brace and glanced over at Angus. "Yeah, I'm good."

"You been burnin' a lot of hours volunteering at the pub. Maybe you need to cut back a little and get your head in the game here. Tired men have more accidents."

"Let's just get this done, brother."

The two men continued working on the half-assembled pergola. They were on a job site booked through Owen. The woman of the house didn't know squat about what it was; she just liked the name and wanted one on her deck. She'd come out several times to bring them lemonade and to ogle the shirtless men as they worked.

"Ms. Carr's been giving you the eye all afternoon. You gonna hit that?"

Patrick pulled a scrap two-by-four and measured another brace to replace the short one. "Nah. Go ahead if you want."

Angus shook his head. "Not my type."

Divorced with too much money to spend and obviously horny. Since when was a woman like that not Angus's type? "Maybe I should ask if you're okay, brother?"

Angus drilled a pilot hole for one of the top beams. "I'm as good as you are."

"Been seeing Rhyleigh?"

"Some."

"Like her?"

"Yeah."

"Fuck, man, you sound like Owen with all the one-word answers. What's going on with you, bro?"

Angus put down the drill. "I've been thinking a lot lately. About life and future and shit like that. We've been side by side for our whole lives and had a lot of good times, but I'm feeling like I need to make some changes. Ones that are only for me. I don't want to piss you off or hurt your feelings, but I've been considering getting my own place. Maybe it's time to be Patrick and Angus, instead of Patrick-n-Angus. Make sense?"

Patrick couldn't help the pinch in his heart. His brother articulated the words he'd been feeling since they pulled up outside of Gallaghers's a few months ago. "Yeah, I get it. I've had a few thoughts about it myself."

"Anything to do with Sloane or is it the pub?"

Patrick brought the chop saw down and the noise provided him with a moment of privacy. The pub meant a lot to him, but where did Sloane fit in? When he spotted Claudio sitting with her the other day, he had the urge to jerk the man from the booth and beat the shit out of him. Sloane's words *"I don't know what you're trying to accomplish, but I don't want any part of it"* had stopped him in his tracks.

At the memory, he thought, *Good*, continuing to check the fitting of the new brace. Somewhere along the way, he'd started thinking about Sloane as his. He didn't know when it had happened. They'd started as friends, then coworkers, and now she'd become an integral part of his life. Being at the pub had turned into his favorite part of the day, however, it was seeing Sloane behind the bar that he looked forward to most.

Her ever-changing hair color and style, her easy talk with patrons, her no-nonsense approach to trouble makers, her smile, her laugh, her teasing, the whole tiny package that was her. He'd gotten sick to his stomach when he'd thought she might ban him from the pub, but in truth, he would never regret the kiss he stole from her. Nor could he forget her reaction to him. The way her lips molded perfectly to his like she was made for him.

"Yo, Patrick! You gonna stare at that piece all damn day or get it in place?"

Patrick flipped off his brother and picked up a hammer and four nails.

"Can you fuck her and walk away?"

Patrick raised his eyes to the sky. He'd done that dozens of times over the years and now the thought of being inside Sloane for one night and then never again sent spikes of pain through his heart. "No. I can't."

"You love her, don't you, brother?"

Yes, he did. He loved her. He loved everything about her, and that realization scared the shit out of him.

Patrick stopped and met his twin's eyes. "Yeah, I

think I do, and I don't have a fuckin' clue what to do about it."

Angus shrugged and tapped the overhead beam into place. "You got two choices. Either tell her and see if she feels the same, or keep your mouth shut and watch her get with someone else."

"What if she doesn't want to be with me like that?"

"Sometimes you gotta risk it all to get what you want."

Chapter Nine

"BOW DOWN, MERE MORTALS! PATRICK MACATEER IS in the hoooouuuse!"

"Fuck," I muttered under my breath as my stomach flipped over. Then I schooled my features into my normal acerbic self. "Yo, Bacchus incarnate! People been askin' for that damn drink of yours all night. Get your ass back here 'cause I ain't servin' that."

The penis colossus had taken a step further down to the gutter and got renamed Patrick's dick by one of the random harem of his that showed up on a regular basis. I didn't know for sure, but I believe it was Reese who started it. She loved coming to the bar and ordering in a loud voice, "I want a tall Patrick's dick." Tall meaning the seven-inch test tube glass, not the six inch. I hated it with a passion, but women kept ordering the damn things with a giggle and the register rang up dozens of them every night.

"You okay, Sloane?" Patrick beamed as he slipped behind the bar. He started wearing black T-shirts with the company logo same as me. It fit tight across his formed pecs and shoulders, and the sleeves barely held his rounded biceps and triceps. I didn't know what it was about a man's triceps that I loved so much but seeing those perfect-shaped muscles made it harder to fight the attraction I had for this man.

Now that I'd seen what laid under that shirt made it harder.

"I'm good. Gordon's gonna come down later after the baby goes to bed."

He nodded and made a humming noise in acknowledgment. Maybe it was my imagination, but he'd been acting funny the last few times he'd been around me. "Anything happening tonight?"

"Nope, just Friday night karaoke and selling booze. The rain will keep some people at home, but your harem is here."

Patrick raspberried me at my harem comment. I raised my eyebrow. "Who else do you think wants that damn dick drink of yours?"

His face split into a wide smile and I braced. "Oh, come now, darlin'. Maybe you should try a Patrick's dick once. You might like it."

The sudden peal of thunder boomed, reflecting my current mood. The clouds opened up and dumped their entire contents on the street outside. I couldn't say why my mood was so damn shitty. Maybe my body was prepping for a sporadic period and maybe I was just in a bad funk. Either way, I had the rare desire for people to drink their drinks and go the fuck home.

Patrick made his concoction and served it to the bevy of women who sat at their usual spot. I did my best to shut off my ears to their squeals at whatever lines Patrick fed them. Jealous? A little, I supposed. It wasn't often anymore that I dreamed about being one of those women at the bar—the ones with the perfect bodies, perfect hair, and perfect lives.

I knew appearances can be deceiving, probably more than most. Plenty of people put on big showy façades to hide what really went on inside. If thoughts were audible, perhaps Reese's inner dialogue was closer to a desperate plea for some-one, anyone to love her. If so, she picked the wrong one as Patrick didn't act like he had any intention of bonding to only one woman. I imagined that after her frequent trips to sit at the bar and make her plays, she went home and cried into her pillow, praying that Patrick would see more in her than a regular customer who liked his drink recipe.

I was glad I'd wised up to that a long time ago. I did, didn't I?

The universe decided to fuck with me tonight. The door opened up and a single customer came in absolutely drenched. Claudio slicked back his soaked hair and caught me looking at him. His face broke into a huge smile and my belly dropped to the floor.

Damnit, why me?

He looked good, even dripping water and forming a puddle under his feet.

Don't go there, Sloane. You already know how that story ended. Time to let bygones be bygones. Simply treat him like any other customer.

I pointed a finger at him and used my sternest voice to hide the tremble in my knees. "Don't move one inch from that spot!"

My loud yell captured the attention of the bar patrons. I picked up several clean hand towels and walked them over to my ex. "Dry yourself before you come any further."

His eyes glowed. "Concerned about me getting pneumonia?"

"More like not having to clean up after your ass. What the hell are you doing out in this shit?"

He laughed and those dulcet tones hit me straight in the heart. God, I used to love that laugh. When I'd had a bad day, all he had to do was smile and let out a few ha-has and I'd be better. It always worked up until it didn't. I thought perhaps he wanted his Wednesday visit to rekindle something.

Not gonna happen.

He scrubbed a towel over his head and face and blotted his clothes with another one. "I photographed a wedding reception a few blocks over and thought I'd stop by for a drink. I didn't plan on walking through a deluge."

I made a noise in my throat. "I suppose not. You're dry enough to come to the bar now."

My head said, *Fake it, fake it, fake it,* as I turned to go back to my customary spot. "Clark, my man!" Patrick greeted him as I took a bottled beer order. "What brings you out tonight?"

The soaked man visibly gritted his teeth. "Claudio. I'm looking for company other than bridezillas and their anxious mothers."

Out of habit, I flipped the tool on my finger a few

times then popped the cap off into the air and batted it into the trash can with the back of the opener. "Tab or pay as you go?"

"Pay as you go."

I took the twenty the guy handed me and made change at the register. Claudio sat at the bar away from the harem as Patrick made him a cranberry vodka. Their conversation wasn't private as they didn't check their volume.

"You getting married?"

"God, no, just taking pics. How that woman got anyone to put a ring on her finger is beyond me. Nothing made her happy. She complained about the color of the flowers not being the right shade of pink. Two tablecloths were uneven in the reception hall. One of the bridesmaids had a shoulder tattoo that showed. The dresses were strapless... need I say more? You name it, she had something to say about it."

Patrick tossed three ice cubes in the air and caught them in a glass as they came down. This wasn't easy as the cubes tended to bounce out and you had to drop the glass a bit as you got them. He'd been practicing this trick for a while and I hadn't been giving him any shit about it. Ice on the floor wasn't that big a deal and he always cleaned up after himself. "I don't get that."

"Get what?"

"Weddings. People spend ten thousand or more on what? Crepe paper and a pretty dress? Useless."

Claudio took a big swallow of the drink and cleared his throat. "Take it easy on weddings, man. That's part of my livelihood now."

"You get paid a lot for taking pictures?"

"Made fifteen hundred tonight. Probably make another six or seven from the people in the wedding party."

"No shit?"

Claudio shook his head.

Patrick whistled through his teeth. "Damn, I'm in the wrong business."

"Change your mind about weddings?"

"As long as it's not mine."

"Hey, Patrick, if you did have a wedding someday, what would it be like?" Reese chimed in. She looked a little miffed to be left out of the conversation.

Patrick put a thoughtful expression on his face. "If I ever fell into the marriage trap, there's only one way I'd ever seal the deal. Vegas. Drive through chapel. Drunk Elvis officiating. The works. I wouldn't even tell my woman we're doing it. I'd just take her there and get it done."

Claudio tipped the last of the drink into his mouth and waved off a second one. "You have one flaw in your plan. Have to have a girlfriend first. Got one?"

A big smile and laugh erupted from Patrick's mouth. "Fuck no, too much hassle."

Claudio and several other people joined in the mirth at Patrick's words, but I could see the devastation on Reese's face. She was more into Patrick than I thought, and for a moment she had my sympathy.

My chest tightened up and the need for solitude hit me with enough force I couldn't breathe. "I'm going in the back to take stock. Holler if you need me."

I didn't bother to look at anyone as I left. The clipboard with the current inventory hung on a peg just inside the storeroom. Cases and kegs stayed in the big walk-in cooler along with other refrigerated ingredients. Liquor boxes and other supplies stacked up on the brand-new wood shelves Patrick and Angus built earlier this week.

There were other updates around the bar that needed to happen. One of the bathrooms needed new stall locks and faucets that didn't drip. Several booth seats had big tears in them. The light over the dartboards partitioned off at the back of the bar tended to flicker from some sort of short. I sighed as I contemplated the never-ending list of work. Tomorrow, I'd call a contractor. It really wasn't fair for me to expect Patrick to do it when he had helped me out so much already.

I went into the humming walk-in and made marks on the page. There were inventory apps I could keep on my phone to use, but I liked using pen and paper. As I counted and wrote down the numbers, the door cracked open behind me.

"Gotta tap a new Killian's keg. Gordon's up front now. You okay back here?" Patrick came in dragging a hand-truck.

"Yeah, I'm good."

He found the right keg and grunted as he tilted it to slip the metal plate under it. The close quarters had him brushing against me. "I noticed you're not happy about Claudio being here. He bothering you again?"

"Not really. We dated a few years back, then he left. That's all."

"Is he trying to win you back?"

The acidic tone in his voice had me looking up from my clipboard. His face was only a hairbreadth away from mine and I saw the striations in his eyes. Bands of green, blue, and teal stared back at me. That now familiar thrill coursed through my middle and I prayed he didn't see any visible reaction from it. "I'm not planning on it, and why should it matter to you?"

"It matters."

"Why?"

"It just does."

His ire got on my last nerve and I let him know it. "You have several dozen women panting after you on a nightly basis, including one sitting out there right now, and you're mad because a man from my past, someone I dated, might be interested in me. Do I have that right?"

"Yeah, you got it right."

I slammed the clipboard down on the keg and opened on him with two barrels. "First of all, the breakup between Claudio and I was messy. Very messy. Not going back for seconds, *ever*. Second, who the fuck do you think you are? My private life is none of your business. If I want to take Claudio upstairs and fuck him for old time's sake, that too, is none of your business. Third... I don't know what third is!"

"No." His growl should have warned me.

"What do you mean 'no'?" I spat.

"No, you're not taking him up to your place to fuck for any reason. Not when you kissed me like you did last week."

My stomach pulled a sharp curve in my middle. "What the hell are you talking about?"

"Confession time, sweetheart. That kiss put a fire in my gut that still burns. Your taste, your sweet lips, I can't get it out of my mind and it's driving me crazy. Every time that asshole comes in here, he watches you with hungry eyes. I want to take him outside and beat the shit out of him. I've never felt like that before about any woman. There could be hundreds of ladies out there, all lined up to be with me, share my bed, be my girlfriend or whatever. Truth is there's only one woman I've ever considered for that title and she's standing right here in front of me. "

My jaw dropped. Of all the words I expected to come out of Patrick's mouth, those were further out than Jupiter.

For the first time in forever, I had nothing. Nada. No witty comebacks. No flippant sentences. No puns or jokes.

I only had action. I raised my hand to grip his neck and pull him down to me. My mouth melded with his as he let go of the hand-truck and it clanged into the keg it held. I swear steam rose from us as we heated up the cold walk-in. Our tongues tangled for a brief moment, then he took over. Heat zapped me to my toes. His breaths, his heartbeats, and his hard want was evident against me as he drew me into himself. It had been a long time since I felt this way. Like someone thought me beautiful and worthy of attention. A heavy ache settled between my legs and I squeezed my thighs together in an attempt to find some relief.

Was it real? Fairy tales and romance novels had happy endings where the guy and girl always triumphed over whatever conflict drove them apart. It wasn't the same in real life. Cinderella didn't always get her prince. I thought I had that happy, pretty fairy ending once, all wrapped up in pretty pink unicorn ribbons. Instead, I got smacked down with a dose of reality that crippled some people forever. I survived, but not without scars, ones I would carry the rest of my existence.

I wasn't immune to handsome men and had done my share of fantasizing when alone in bed and even pictured Patrick a time or two when I played with my vibrator. But having him in the flesh, kissing me, touching me, desiring me; I imagined how good it would feel to have that hard dick pressing against my stomach slide inside me. Fuck, I wanted it so bad I could cry. Could I dare take a chance? Should I risk it all on the hope that someone could actually care about me? Perhaps even love me?

A whimper escaped from my throat as his hand moved from the ball of my shoulder to my collarbone. His hand started drifting downward to my chest, and I froze up.

Not yet! Not yet! I'm not ready!

I tore my mouth away from him and painfully gasped in the frigid air. "Patrick, I need—"

A loud banging on the walk-in door had both of us jumping apart. "Patrick, we need that keg ASAP, man. You need help in there?"

Gordon's voice chilled us quicker than the temperature of the giant refrigerator. Patrick pulled back and his warm breath caressed my lips as he called back, "I got it. Be right there."

"You seen Sloane?"

"Bathroom."

"Oh, okay. See you up front."

Patrick's eyes glittered at me. "This isn't over, darlin'. I'll come up to your place after the bar closes, yeah?"

Panic filled every cell in my body. "No, you can't."

Confusion crossed his face. "Why not?"

"You just can't."

His took my hand and placed it on his stiff dick. My fingers curled around that thick hard length as he gripped it with me. "Feel that? This is for you. This is what you do to me every night I come here."

"Please, let me go." *Fuck, could I sound any more pleading?*

"I bet if I put my hand down your pants, I'd find your pussy soaked."

"Patrick."

"This wouldn't be for one night, baby. I've never said this to any woman before, but when I look at you, I see a future. I see someone who makes me want to settle down and be in one place. I see a woman who sets my blood racing just with the thought of being with her. I see someone I could love, maybe for the long haul. I know you don't think I have staying power, and for most of my life, you'd be right. But this is the first time I've ever met a woman I wanted to stay with at all. Please, let me come up later and I'll show you how serious I am."

"I can't."

"Why not?"

I was on the verge of sobbing. I still had his dick in my hand, and I jerked it away. "No, I can't... I just can't yet... I...."

"Sloane, please fucking tell me why."

My turned-on buzzing body screamed at me to take the risk, and my overwhelmed head trumpeted to retreat and regroup.

I chose the latter.

Tears filled my eyes as I shrunk into a babbling incoherent version of myself. "I can't tell you.... Please let me go. I can't think.... I can't— No!"

I fled. There's no other word for it. Me, Sloane, Gallaghers's tough feisty bartender and business owner, ran from the man I wanted more than anyone else.

He yelled my name as I pushed out of the refrigerator and scrabbled at the locked door to the staircase leading to the upper floors. I didn't stop until I reached my apartment and walked out on the roof deck. I clutched myself and let it out. This wasn't a pretty cry. This was hard, wracking sobs that erupted out of me with volcanic force. My throat burned with the effort and I gagged several times. *Why me? Why why why why?*

Eventually, the tempest inside me calmed, and I curled up to sniffle and spasm on one of the long lounge chairs, not caring that the wet from the rain soaked into my clothes. My phone chirped with several texts from both Gordon and Patrick. I couldn't bear to read the ones from Patrick, but I did answer my brother.

Gordon: You okay, sis?

Me: I'm fine. Just not feeling too hot. I'm gonna take the rest of the night. You good with closing?

The dots bounced around for a bit.

Gordon: Yeah, Patrick and I got this. You sure you're okay?

Me: Promise.

Gordon: You'd tell me if something's wrong, right?

Me: Yes, and nothing is wrong. I just need a break.

Gordon: I get that. Patrick and me got this. Don't worry. Talk tomorrow, yeah?

Me: Sure.

Three more chirps added more texts from Patrick as I turned off my phone. Tears kept leaking from my eyes as I gazed out on the city. I swiped my arm across my nose, not caring about the mess I made. My brain ran the same pattern of thought over and over again like one of those crazy joke flow charts that recycled the reader back to the beginning on every path.

Patrick likes you and works at the bar. Tell him and see what he does. He stays, or he leaves. Don't tell him and see what he does. He stays, or he leaves. Get mad and tell him it's none of his business. He stays, or he leaves. Trust him with the truth. He stays, or he leaves.

My temples pounded, making my stuffed nose worse. I could tell my eyes had swollen up and were probably red from me rubbing at them. The rain had left the night cooler than normal, and I shivered. I went back down into my apartment to take a painkiller and to get my thickest quilt. Not ready to shower and go to bed, I wrapped up in the quilt and laid down on my sofa in its cocooning warmth. I didn't intend to fall asleep as I thought myself too wound up for it, but I did.

Chapter Ten

PATRICK PULLED INTO THE PARKING AREA AND TURNED off his truck. His mouth formed a hard and determined line as he stared up at Sloane's floor through the windshield. After he and Gordon closed down the bar last night, he'd left her alone and gone home himself. He'd spent the rest of the night staring at the cracks in the ceiling with his hands behind his head. Over and over again he went over their conversation in his mind, looking for flaws in what he'd said or done.

"I can't."

"Why not?"

"No, I can't... I just can't yet... I..."

"Sloane, please fucking tell me why?"

"I can't tell you.... Please let me go. I can't think.... I can't— No!"

He figured it couldn't be another man as he'd been at the bar often enough he would have noticed or heard someone say something. Claudio? Not him. The bastard acted possessive sometimes like he wanted to get back with Sloane, but so far he'd seen no evidence she reciprocated it.

The bar? Impossible. Gordon said the bar's finances were good. Not great, but good. He'd even floated the idea of bringing him on full-time.

Patrick had been surprised as hell at the time, but when Gordon explained about the restaurant idea and Cammie's excitement, plus that they'd already been looking at a house over toward Swannanoa close to her parents, the offer had left its mark. The couple's plan was to tag team working until their daughter, Courtney, started kindergarten. Then they planned to hire someone to work the nights and some weekends.

Gordon had gone on to say that his daughter's life would be nine to five, Monday to Friday once she started school, and he and Cammie wanted to get their lives scheduled as close to that as possible. He didn't blame him for not wanting his daughter raised by a bunch of sitters while Gordon poured drinks until midnight every night and Cammie decorated fancy plates for rich people.

Gordon had been adamant that he thought they could make the changes happen, and as soon as they did, he was out of the bar business. And Patrick? Apparently, he was the perfect replacement.

Patrick grabbed the bag of cinnamon rolls fresh from the bakery and two coffees. At 9:00 a.m., he should have been at the job site with Owen and Angus, but he'd begged off as this was more important. He planned on trapping Sloane and hashing things out, one way or another.

The more he thought about Gordon's proposal last night, the more he wanted it. His stomach churned at the thought of taking the plunge. Never in his wildest fantasies had he ever thought he would face this decision. He'd believed for years that he'd spend his entire life traveling around the country, working jobs with his twin and family. He wasn't stupid enough to think he'd be able to do that forever as eventually, his body would break down from all the hard, physical labor, but he imagined that would happen decades from now. The last few months, hell, the last few years, showed him different, and his eyes opened to new possibilities. All three of his older brothers found partners for life.

Women totally devoted to them and their growing families.

What he saw when he looked at Connor, Owen, and Garrett was more than just happiness. Much more. Every time he visited with them, he found them filled with contentment, satisfaction, and sheer joy in their lives. It showed in the look of delight on Owen's face as he smiled at Melanie while juggling baby Ryan in his arms. It showed in Garrett's glee when he designed another expansion project for the Bed and Breakfast Inn he and Bertie ran together. It showed in the pride Connor took when he watched his wife get named teacher of the year, or when any of his step-kids won a school award.

Patrick balanced the cardboard drink tray in one hand as he keyed in the lock combo. The door clicked, and he entered the back office space. The second door to the upper apartments stayed locked, but he also knew that combo. Gordon mentioned one night that his birthday was the code to the outer door and Sloane's birthday opened the inner.

Patrick pressed the buttons he knew by heart and heard the door lock disengage. He took a huge breath and let it out slowly. Last time he'd climbed these steps, he'd done so with Angus to measure Gordon's apartment and get some ideas for the future renovation. He'd never been in Sloane's unit at all.

A lump rose in his throat as he stared up the dimly lit steps. Fuck how the hell did men do this shit?

Morning, Sloane. Wanna be my girlfriend?

Hi, I think we should date.

Can I put my tongue in your pussy?

All sorts of phrases came to his mind as he climbed the steps. His work boots sounded dull echoes through the stairwell.

Never had he been in this situation before—one where he had no control over the outcome. Love 'em and leave 'em had been his modus operandi until now. He finally acknowledged the truth about the trail of broken hearts he left behind him everywhere he'd gone and regretted it. He wished he could go back and ask forgiveness for the callous way he'd used so many. For the first time in his life, he found himself on the potential receiving end of rejection. His plan was to bring breakfast and lay his heart in Sloane's hands, in the hope that she would give him a chance. She could just as well take it and rip it into pieces before throwing him out of her life permanently.

He stood before her door, his heart pounding,

head spinning, and gut churning. Two deep breaths and he knocked.

Nothing. No peephole either.

Patrick frowned, thinking he needed to put one in for her. He knocked again and waited.

Still nothing.

His hand tested the knob and found the door unlocked.

"Christ, the woman is nuts." He walked into the apartment with the idea to start off the morning with a safety lecture. *Yeah, that would be a good icebreaker before we get to the heavy shit.*

The apartment had the potential of being a steampunk dream—lofted ceiling with industrial ductwork, red brick walls with big windows, and completely open space. The small kitchen area had semi-modern appliances and the sitting area had a couch and flat-screen TV on an entertainment center, otherwise the place appeared cavernous.

Not even the bedroom was partitioned off. Patrick took in the rumpled sheets. A colorful quilt laid crumpled up on the couch and he surmised she slept there last night. Why? Another question to ask her. A sectioned off room close to the back wall had to be the bathroom. It made sense as he spotted the array of pipes adorning the ceiling. The natural light from the windows cast a harsh glare, and he took several steps into the apartment to get a better look at everything. What met his eyes blew confusion into his brain.

"What the fuck?" he muttered under his breath.

A row of wigs on Styrofoam heads lined a shelf mounted above the dresser. Blonde with green tips, Brunette with long waves, one with tight black braids, the multi-colored one he's seen her wear for Cinco de Mayo, another one in long blonde curls, even the *Star Wars* Rae-styled one.

A shuffling noise sounded, and he stood stock-still as Sloane came from behind the partition. Obviously, she had been in the shower when he knocked earlier and hadn't heard him. The lecture about putting in a peephole and the dangers of leaving her door unlocked died from his lips as he took in her appearance in utter shock.

She stood before him in all her naked glory, not quite bony, but definitely skinny. Small thighs, slim hips, tiny waist, thin arms.

"Sweet Jesus, Mary, and Joseph." His whisper sounded loud in the silence.

And a completely bald head plus two horizontal scars where her breasts were supposed to be.

THE LIGHT STREAMING THROUGH THE TALL WINDOWS woke me up with a cramp in my neck and a line of dried drool across my chin. Fuck, I fell asleep on my sofa after all. I clicked off the muted TV as I gingerly rose, my back locking up in protest. Damn, I needed to get my ass over to the yoga studio. I arched, trying to stretch the tension from my muscles, but the painful protest had me bending over like an old lady.

Coffee. I needed coffee, but first, a hot shower since I didn't get one last night. I shuffled into my bathroom and stripped, letting the clothes land on the floor. I had a hamper in the corner but bending over to grab my stuff proved to be more than I could handle. No one lived here but me and seldom did anyone visit other than Gordon, Cammie, and Courtney.

You could have had Patrick up here last night, my inner voice mocked.

Gah, why did that thought have to crop up? I started the shower and sat on the plastic bench I'd placed in here. The huge tiled space had no curtain or door as I never saw the need to put one up. I had a gorgeous view of the toilet and sink vanity on one side, and the claw-footed tub and linen shelves on the other. The extra-wide shower head mounted directly above me poured steaming water over my head and back, and my groan echoed against the walls.

Wonder what Patrick would think of your shower design?

Stop it, Sloane!

He's not as shallow as you think.

Doesn't matter. It's not going to happen.

You should tell him.

I can't risk it.

He might surprise you.

I might also be devastated.

I shook my head to clear the voices arguing inside it. *Fuck, the man had me talking to myself.*

When my neck released enough to stand, I reached for my favorite body wash and squidgie-thingie. The ginger-orange scent never failed to give me a boost. I needed every bit of positive I could find. At some point, I had to talk to Patrick, and that terrified me. What was I supposed to say?

I really like you, but I have this situation.

Maybe we should just be friends. No more kissing.

Can we fuck with our clothes on so you don't have to look at me?

I had no clue what to do, but thankfully I had some time to think before seeing him tonight. Maybe he would stay home or go somewhere else for a change. I could dream, right?

I ran a hand over my head to check for stubble and reached for the shaving cream and razor. My hair didn't grow back as I'd hoped. It came up in random patches in some areas and nothing in others. What did grow back was thin and brittle, unlike the rich chocolate it used to be. I decided to just keep it shaved unless it all came back uniform.

I still waited, even after these past few years.

I swiped my hand across the fogged mirror to clear it and assess the damage last night's crying had left me. My eyelids were still puffy and slightly red. Hopefully they would go down enough to apply false lashes later. Coloring in my wispy eyebrows could wait too. One advantage I supposed was the lack of leg and arm hair. No pubes either.

I didn't pay any attention to my surroundings as I left my bathroom and sauntered buck naked into my sleeping area. No need to call it a bedroom as there weren't any other walls in my place. I supposed I could be concerned about the windows, but from this angle, all you could see was the sky. Since I couldn't see the other buildings, the other buildings couldn't see me, right? Frankly, who would want to? One look at my breastless chest would scare off any Peeping Toms.

My mind listed tasks for the day to keep from thinking about Patrick and what to say to him. *Get the inventory done, make the orders, pick up groceries, run the reports, and get the books caught up, get the deposits ready—*

"Sweet Jesus, Mary, and Joseph."

My stomach dropped through the floor like an anchor. Patrick stood in my apartment in front of me, two coffees in one hand and a bakery bag in the other.

I stopped breathing.

For a split second, we just stared. His face was slack with shock and mine with humiliation.

He saw.

He saw *everything*.

There was nothing close by to cover myself. I put my hands over my chest, but that left my pussy exposed. But if shifted my hands down, my scars were visible. Nowhere to run. Bathroom? I'd get trapped in there, and if I knew Patrick MacAteer the way I thought I did, he'd come after me. I resorted to crouching down, hunching over to hide as much of me as possible, and gasping as I started to breathe again. *Fight or flight? No way out, so fight it is.*

"What the fuck are you doing here? Get the fuck out! Get out! Get out! Get OUT!"

My screech reverberated through my apartment as I clawed at the top sheet on my bed for some sort of cover.

"Go! Go! Go!"

The windows in my place should have shattered at the decibels coming from me.

Patrick remained routed, staring as I screamed. He watched as I fell apart. I picked up a tennis shoe near my bed and chucked it at him.

"Get out! Now!"

It didn't reach him, and he didn't move so I picked up another one and threw it harder. This one hit him in the stomach. I was sure it didn't hurt that hard washboard of his, but the impact did cause him to drop the coffees and the bag. Brown liquid spewed over the hardwood floor and I looked around for something else to throw.

"Get the fuck out!"

He turned away. God in heaven, he turned and walked away from me.

I died.

My heart shattered so hard the pain sent me to

the floor. I went blind, it hurt so bad. My hands curled into fists as I resisted the urge to tear at my flesh. I was beyond crying, taking in huge gasps of air and screaming silently in my head. The pressure built to the point I needed to scream for real or explode.

My world spun as the heavy quilt I'd left on my sofa came down over me and I got scooped up in two arms. Two strong arms that encircled me, my back to his front. Two arms that no matter how hard I scraped at them to let me go, banded me in solid steel. Two arms that held me still until I stopped struggling.

"Calm." Patrick's rough command huffed close to my ear. "Breathe with me, baby. In over four, hold, and out over four. Ready? Follow me."

I had no choice but to do as he said. I drew in a choppy breath, smelling his woodsy cologne and held it. His exhale tickled my ear as I aped him.

"Again."

My bowstring tight body started shaking, but he kept his grip on me. Another breath. Then another. And another. I stopped fighting him, but that didn't make the pain in my heart or the panic in my mind go away. The way he held me, fuck, what I wouldn't give for this to be real. "You can let go now." *Please don't!*

"I can, but I'm not going to. Breathe with me."

The sundial clock on my wig shelf clicked through ten minutes before the iron grip around me relaxed a bit, but he still didn't release me.

"Cancer." He made this as a statement, not a question.

I couldn't hide it from him now. Best just to put it all out there and let the chips fall.

"Four years ago. Double mastectomy. Six weeks of chemo and radiation therapy. One more year, and I'll move up to the status of a cancer-free survivor." I sniffed as the tears broke free and fell. "I'm also one of the statistics in that my hair never grew back right and at this point probably never will."

"I wondered how you changed hairstyles all the time."

"It wasn't supposed to happen this way. The doctor found a small lump during a regular exam that turned out to be malignant. Just one little lump. The surgery was supposed to be an isolated spot on my left breast. Not supposed to be a big deal." My words tumbled out in a rush to escape and free themselves. "There would be some scarring and some reduction in breast size," but I could get some cosmetic surgery later and even things out."

The heat from his body flowed through the quilt, warming my back. His chin rested on my shoulder and I was acutely aware of my naked state next to him. His voice rumbled against my neck, sending sparks down my spine. "Finish it."

"When they got in there, they found the tissue riddled with cancer all over my chest and made the call to take them. I woke up afterwards with Gordon by my side and I remember holding his hand while he told me I lost both breasts."

My breath hitched. Once my word vomit started, I couldn't stop it. "Claudio and I... we'd just got engaged when I found the lump. He stuck around during the surgery part, but after... he couldn't look at me the same way. The chemo was pretty damn rough. The hair loss, constantly sick, smelling like vomit all the time. He took a job taking pictures on a cruise ship and used that as his excuse for breaking up with me, but I know the truth. His view of me changed. He didn't see me as a woman anymore and couldn't handle getting saddled with someone he would never desire again. He couldn't see past my scars and accept me in my new body."

"You still love him?" A squeeze punctuated his soft growl.

I shook my head. "No. I don't blame him, I suppose, but he abandoned me when I needed him the most. Gordon and Cammie took care of me as well as they could, but I still spent most of my recovery and chemo time alone. There was a lot of pain, both physical and mental. I didn't have time to prepare for the possibility of losing my breasts and I'm still... I'm not over it yet. I don't know that I ever will be. I've been saving up for cosmetic surgery, but the most it will do is look right. I'll never feel the same again."

My voice grew hoarser and my eyes swelled up from crying again. "I've been scared out of my mind that it would happen again with you. Claudio saw me as only half a woman. I felt like only half a woman. I'm scared to death you'll see me in that way too, and I don't think I can recover from that level of rejection again. It damn near killed me the first time when the person I fell in love with walked away. I can't do it again."

"You love me." I didn't have to look at him to hear the smile in his voice.

"Yes, dammit, I do, and I'm terrified of it. I've tried to let it go or talk myself out of it, but then you walk in the pub every night with the big announce- ment of your presence and I melt. It fucking killed me every time I saw you make those damn Patrick's dicks for your adoring masses. Reese with her perfect whole body and size double Ds. I've been jealous for weeks."

He released his breath in a warm sigh against my neck. "Thank God."

Pain pierced my chest. I jerked in his arms, and he tightened up.

"No, baby, not like that. Thank God you love me. I may be a prick for saying this, but I'm glad you said it first. Makes it easier for me to say it."

"Say what?"

"I love you, Sloane." He barked a wry laugh. "Fuck, I've never said that before to a woman I'm not related to. Never felt this for anyone and never wanted to, but seeing you at the bar every night, working so damn hard... fuck me, I don't have the words to describe what it does to me."

His voice broke. He sniffed loudly, swallowed, and let out a shaky breath. I could hardly believe it, but Patrick MacAteer cried against my neck. "Half a woman? Bull-fucking-shit. After going through that hell and beating it, you're too much woman for that asshole. He's half a man for leaving you, and I'm sorry to say this 'cause I know you got hurt bad, but I'm so fucking glad he did. Leaves my path wide open."

The sudden release of the knots in my gut, nearly sent me to my knees. I had no clue of the tension that had built up in my mind and body. I felt almost giddy.

He shifted and placed a soft kiss just below my ear. "Be with me, Sloane. Be my woman."

His lips sent more sparks through me and raised gooseflesh all over my back. It would be so easy to give in and accept his comfort, but I needed to know. "What happens if you change your mind next week?"

He chuckled, and the sound buzzed down my spine. "I'm not changing my mind, baby. Think I've ever had to work this hard before? If you banned me after I kissed you that first time, I was going to camp out in the parking lot and sing cheesy love songs to you until you changed your mind."

I let out my own little laugh to cover my roiling emotions. I wanted so much to believe this was true. "You think that shit works on me?"

"Probably not, but it would have annoyed you so much you'd let me back in just to get me to stop." He nipped at my neck and I shivered. "I mean it, Sloane. Be my woman."

I felt so fucking light I could float and the only thing anchoring me was Patrick's arms. He loved me. He truly, completely, thoroughly loved me. "Okay."

His mouth curled up in a big smile against me and he took my earlobe in his teeth. "I swear I'll be the best boyfriend you've ever had, and if this stays the way I want it to, I'll be the last boyfriend too. I have another serious question to ask you, sweetheart."

"What's that?"

"Can I put my tongue in your pussy now?"

Chapter Eleven

Before I finished nodding and laughing, I found myself stripped of the quilt and in my bed on my back with a seriously turned-on Patrick above me. He twisted his hips to settle between my legs and supported his weight on his forearms as he hovered over me. I barely got in a breath before his lips were on mine in a possessive kiss. He teased me with his tongue until I opened to him. He swept inside, laying claim.

"I love you, Sloane. So fucking much."

He kissed me thoroughly, stroking the inside of my lips, tangling with my tongue, thrusting in and out as if making love to my mouth. I writhed against him as I grew hotter.

"I love your wigs. You look so good when you

change styles and colors. Makes me hard thinking of all the role-playing we can do. You can be Princess Leia and I can be Han Solo. Wanna see my lightsaber?"

I couldn't help but giggle. He moved to my neck, sucking in the skin and licking the sensitive cord until I squealed.

He reared back and looked at me with boyish glee. "You said you lost all your hair, right, even down there?"

He saw it, didn't he? "Um... there's a little fuzz."

"Bare pussy with no razor burn? I gotta see this."

He slid down and pulled my knees wider apart. "Damn, that's beautiful."

My skin flushed red as his heated gaze landed on my open mound. "I don't... eeyah!"

A thousand volts hit me as that magic tongue of his started at the top of my slit and stroked down over my clit to my opening and back. He did it a second time, and the sensation was just as electrifying as the first. The third time had me yelling again.

"Lost your voice, love? Need some words? Try 'ooh, Patrick, that feels so good, Patrick, give me more, Patrick.'"

He punctuated each sentence with a flick of his tongue against my straining clit.

"Patrick, do you always talk this much?" I gasped out on a half-laugh.

"You're right. Let's get down to the business of making you scream my name when you come."

Down to business indeed.

He licked, sucked, twirled and teased, turning me into one big oversensitive writhing mass. At one point he sucked me into his mouth and fluttered his tongue over the tip of my clit until I thought I would pass out. Every nerve ending fired with pleasure, and the control I had over my body disappeared. It was too much. I tried to push his head away to take a break, but he grabbed my wrists and held them to my hips as his tongue circled round and round.

"Patrick!"

"Wanna come?"

"Yes!"

"Say, Patrick, my love, please let me come'"

"Patrick my love, please...ahh... please let me come."

"Say, Patrick, I love the way you eat my pussy."

"Patrick, I love the way you eat my pussy.'"

"Say, Patrick—"

"Patrick MacAteer, I love you, now finish the job!"

He sucked me back in and pressed his tongue in firm strokes. He let go of one hand and slid a finger inside my channel. It pointed at my belly button and he stroked in and out, spreading slickness everywhere. Even if I had any control left, I couldn't stop the avalanche of pleasure that washed over me. I came, riding wave after wave, my body spasming under his, and I screamed with release.

His finger withdrew from my clasping channel, and I fell in a boneless heap back onto the bed. I vaguely heard him move around as he stripped out of his clothes. As he came back over me, I got a full view of the bottom half of his tattoo. A winking naked Lucky Charms cartoon leprechaun straddled Patrick's erect dick with the words *Magically Delicious.*

I couldn't help it. I touched a finger to the tattoo and burst into laughter.

Patrick grinned down at me. "Got drunk one night with Owen and Garrett. I thought it was a good idea at the time."

He tore open a condom wrapper with his teeth and sheathed himself. I suddenly grew self-conscious and covered my chest with my hands.

"None of that, precious." He pulled them away and to my utter amazement, leaned over and kissed the pink lines, tracing each one with his tongue. "You're beautiful, and I'm one damn lucky man to be here with you."

Tears welled in my eyes. His acceptance filled me with such feeling I thought I would burst apart with joy.

"You forgot something, sweetheart."

"What?"

The hard knob of his dick pushed against my opening. He smiled and made a *tsking* noise "You were supposed to scream my name. We gotta start all over again."

Chapter Twelve

GALLAGHERS'S PUB WAS NOT JUST A PLACE TO BE tonight. It was *the* place to be. Patrick felt lighter, happier, and more carefree than ever. He couldn't stop smiling and several regulars remarked on his demeanor.

"You look like the cat that got the cream."

"Dude, what the hell's got you in such a good mood?"

"Whatever you're mixin', man, I'm buyin'."

"I'm high on life, brothers. Just high on life!"

Sloane stood awkwardly at the register and Patrick grinned even bigger at her slightly open stance. He leaned over to whisper in her ear. "Sore, baby?"

She shot him a scowl. "Don't touch me."

He chuckled. "I'm sorry, sweetheart. I promise I'll

kiss it and make it all better. No sex in four years, eh? Did the soak in the bathtub help?"

She rang up another tab. "It did, until you joined me. By the way, I wasn't completely sexless. I have BOB."

"Who's Bob?

"Battery Operated Boyfriend."

Patrick's smile spread even further. "You have a vibrator? Fuck yeah, baby, you, me, and BOB are gonna have a threesome sometime soon."

Sloane bit her lip to hide her own smile. Patrick laughed and smacked a kiss at her temple before going to take another order. He learned enough drinks and repeated enough tricks that many of them were automatic. He could work, tease, and talk while his mind stayed occupied on other things, mainly Sloane and their morning sex marathon.

His dick ached as he slid it back and forth along Sloane's tight channel. When the head breached, he wanted to weep at her surrounding warmth. Bit by bit, he pushed in and out, coating himself in her juices until he fully seated himself inside her. The gasps, groans, and whimpers from her throat as he claimed her sounded in his ears.

"Am I hurting you, baby?"

"No, it's just been a really long time."

"How long?"

"F-Four years. Ah!"

"Damn, Sloane. You won't ever have to wait that long again, darlin'. Hell, four days will be too much. Maybe four hours. We got a lot of catching up to do."

He pulled out of her slickness and pushed back in, feeling the grip of her body caressing his length. "Beautiful, sweetheart, and a real honor you chose me to be here with you. I promise I'm gonna treasure and take care of this gift you've given me but, fair warning, I want you to be standing at that bar tonight, still feeling me inside you. I want you to come so many times, that everything else is a shadow memory. I want you to be so addicted to me, you can't get enough and never want me to leave."

Her hips moved with him and she clutched at his shoulders, her fingers digging in as he steadily stroked in and out of her body. Glazed eyes met his, and she panted. "I think I'm already there."

"Not yet, baby. But you will be." He prodded inside her at different angles until Sloane gasped sharply and clenched around his pulsing dick. He grinned from ear to ear. "Found it."

"What? Oh, God!" she cried and clenched again as he pressed the same area.

"Your G-spot, darlin'. Now we can really get down to business."

His thrusts became more purposeful as he teased her, sometimes targeting the newly discovered spot and sometimes giving her a minute to catch her breath. He fought the urge to pound into her like a battering ram, as his need to come grew with every push, but his desire to draw out her pleasure proved greater. Her gasps and cries sounded like music as they filled the air and he reveled in them as he leaned down to kiss her.

"That's it, sweetheart. Fuck, you feel so damn good. Love this, baby. Love you."

She writhed against him as she pushed her hips up to meet his next drive. "Do you always talk this much?"

"No, but with you, I have lots to say. Love your taste, baby, and I'm gonna eat you every chance I get. Love to see your mouth on me while I'm doing it. Love this tight pussy of yours, and I can't wait to see how many ways I can take you. Fast and hard, ramming into you from behind. Slow and steady, like we are now in missionary. You on top and I can work your clit. Reverse cowgirl and I'll watch that ass while you ride."

She let out a yell as he increased his speed and drove harder at her spot. Her answering spasm nearly made him spill. He kissed her again, teasing her lips with his tongue. "I can't wait to stop using condoms. Haven't done ungloved yet. Ever. Want to feel all of you, baby."

"Talk... Ooh... Later... Oh!"

"Ever done any ass play? I hope you'll let me do that too."

"God, Patrick!"

"Like that idea, don't you? Your pussy just hugged me."

"Oh! Ah! Fuck! Please, Patrick!"

He kissed her again. "Okay, darlin'. I've got you." He leaned over and lightly bit the side of her neck, enough to let her feel the grip with his teeth. He began thrusting hard and fast at her spot. Her answering scream told him she was there. Her body lost control as her orgasm hit her. Wave after wave gripped him and he pounded through it and his balls tightened up with his own imminent pleasure.

"Ahhhh! Sloane!" He let out a yell to join hers.

"Yo, dude! Wake up, man. Can I get a Guinness and a shot?"

Patrick shook himself and hoped the boner he just sprung wasn't too visible in his jeans. "Got it."

"Distracted much?" Sloane smirked at him.

"Your fault, darlin'. I used three condoms before you finally yelled my name."

She made a noise between a grunt and a groan and Patrick threw back his head and laughed.

Karaoke started and a line of singers paraded across the stage to try to wow the crowd with their talents. Some were hits, and some were misses, but the atmosphere of the place stayed upbeat and fun.

"You've been up with my sister all day, haven't you?" Gordon came down to help with the rush. "Heard some serious shit coming from overhead."

Patrick's mood dampened a little as he took in the serious look on Gordon's face. He recognized brother-protection mode and didn't blame Gordon for his concern. "Yes, I did, and I'm going to be doing it often. Sloane and I are together now and if I have my way, we're going to stay together for a long time. That's not a problem, is it?"

Gordon kept the firm line of his mouth for several tense seconds, then burst into a big smile and laughed. "'Bout damn time. Congrats, brother, although I have to tell you, if you hurt her, I'll take a hammer to your knees. I thought about that with the dickhead she used to be engaged to, but Cammie wouldn't let me."

"No worries there, my friend. I love Sloane, and I'll cut off my right nut before I cause her any more pain than she's already had. Speaking of dickheads, guess who just came in."

Claudio entered with his usual grace. His eyes spotted Sloane at the bar and he seated himself as close to her as possible. He smiled at her and ordered something. Patrick saw red as the man stared openly at her ass when she turned away.

"Hey, I need Patrick's dick extra strong tonight!" Reese had arrived as well with her gaggle of girls.

"Need to shut that shit down, man."

Patrick didn't know which situation Gordon referred to, but either way, he was right. He climbed on the bar and raised both arms in the air as his voice carried over the noise. "Attention, mere mortals! I have a big announcement to make!"

All eyes shifted to the spectacle he made. Even the karaoke singers paused and Pete muted the machine.

"Hear ye, hear ye, people of Gallaghers's Pub. Patrick's dick is no longer on the menu. That recipe now belongs exclusively to my girlfriend, Sloane."

Applause and cheers rang out as he jumped off and strode to Sloane. She was doing her best to seem stern and miffed, but her lips curled into a beaming smile. She chose the long curling black wig tonight, and he reached out to tweak a hanging lock. "This one reminds me of Wonder Woman. I'll play Superman and you can tie me up with your golden lasso."

She didn't hide her wince. "After this morning's session, I need a few days."

"You can always get up close and personal with me lucky charm."

Sloane growled and he laughed as she snapped a towel at his ass. He took her in his arms and carefully placed his hand on the back of her head as to not dislodge the wig. "No problem, baby. I'm not going anywhere. We got lots of time."

Her eyes softened and shone with extra wet. He grinned at her. "I love you, Sloane, every fucking inch. We got a whole new life ahead of us, sweetheart, and I'm down for a full one."

Catcalls, whoops, and whistles filled the air as he laid a long claiming kiss on her in front of a hundred or more people. This time, instead of slapping him, she reached down and grabbed double handfuls of his butt. The crowd roared with approval.

***

Enjoyed Patrick and Sloane's story? In that case, be sure to check out the final book in the series, *Give It To Me*—Angus MacAteer's sweet and sexy story.

A woman with secret desires, an alpha construction worker who enjoys his darker cravings, and a chance meeting that will change every-

thing. Join bestselling author ML Nystrom in the Dragon Runners MC spin-off following the much-loved MacAteer Brothers.

Check out the complete Dragon Runners MC series, too, starting with the incredible *Mute*.

Looking for a new motorcycle romance to check out? *Doc T*, a sexy motorcycle book in Skye McNeil's Macha MC universe, is now available.

Acknowledgments

Big thank-yous to the people who have always been there to help me through the writing process. Brittany Alexander, Whitney Pogue, Alice Woods, Virginia Gaylor, Barbara Hoover, and the incredible Becky Johnson, along with the whole crew at Hot Tree Publishing. Each round of red pen notes teaches me more and more about this word craft, and I look forward each new book to more.

Breast cancer is ugly. No other word for it. The two women mentioned in the dedication are friends who have dealt with breast cancer and survived it. They don't know each other, as one is a college buddy and the other is a former student of mine when I taught at a university. Their only connection is through me and that they both dealt with this nasty demon. I thought about them a lot when I planned this book's outline and at the time, I myself had a breast biopsy to check for a potential problem. I'm glad to say my test was negative, and I'm sorry to say my friends had positive ones. Both ladies went through surgeries, chemo, and a lot of mental and physical stress, but they faced this life-changing disease with smiles, jokes, and as much joyous laughter as they could. I admire them greatly for their strength and perseverance.

Survival of this particular cancer is very high, but you have to find it early. Ladies, go treat yourself to a fun-filled mammogram. In the midst of your careers, daily tasks, families, and all the work you do for everyone around you, please don't forget to take care of yourselves.

Thanks for reading *Risk It All.* I do hope you enjoyed Patrick and Sloane's story. I appreciate your help in spreading the word, including telling a friend. Before you go, it would mean so much to me if you would take a few minutes to write a review and share how you feel about my story so others may find my work. Reviews really do help readers find books. Please leave a review on your favorite book site.

Don't miss out on New Releases, Exclusive Give-aways and much more!
Join my newsletter: https://www.mlnystrom.com/contact
Visit my website for my current booklist: https://www.mlnystrom.com/

I'd love to hear from you directly, too. Please feel free to email me at melody @mlnystrom.com or check out my website https://www.mlnystrom.com/ for updates.

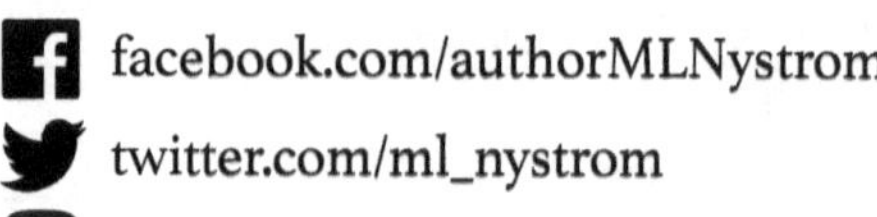

facebook.com/authorMLNystrom

twitter.com/ml_nystrom

instagram.com/mlnystrom

Hot Tree Publishing opened its doors in 2015 with an aspiration to bring quality fiction to the world of readers. With the initial focus on romance and a wide spread of romance subgenres, Hot Tree Publishing has since opened their first imprint, Tangled Tree Publishing, specializing in crime, mystery, suspense, and thriller.

Firmly seated in the industry as a leading editing provider to independent authors and small publishing houses, Hot Tree Publishing is the sister company to Hot Tree Editing, founded in 2012. Having established in-house editing and promotions, plus having a well-respected market presence, Hot Tree Publishing endeavors to be a leader in bringing quality stories to the world of readers.

Interested in discovering more amazing reads brought to you by Hot Tree Publishing? Head over to the website for information:

www.hottreepublishing.com